JUST FREDDY

By Joel Stern

First Published in the United Kingdom in 2022.

First Edition 2022.

ISBN: 9798408001705

This book is for

Ethan, Koby, Marnie, Samuel

and the future generations.

CONTENTS

In loving memory of

Alfred 'Freddy' Stern

1925 - 2020

FOREWORD
BY ROB RINDER

The most profound truths of human life are always expressed in the simplest ways. In 1905 George Santayana remarked that *"Those who cannot remember the past are condemned to repeat it."* His words were a stark warning that unless we teach our children about humanity's dark capacity for hatred, our world would be doomed to a never-ending cycle of violence and conflict. These words were written at the start of a century that saw us descend into indescribable human depravity. They were a prophesy. We did not listen to them then and we have failed to hear them today where I sit, writing in the comfort of my home, as the shadow of genocide, racism and prejudice in all its grotesque forms endures with tragic strength.

His words resonate within me every day of my life. They are personal. My grandfather survived the Holocaust. His parents, brother and four sisters (the youngest was seven years old) were all murdered in Treblinka extermination camp. Their journey to death did not happen in a sudden explosion of violence nor in some uncivilised place or time. The twisted roots of their horrifying end formed under the earth of the most forward thinking advanced liberal state at the time. People there had grown safe in the belief that democracy would surely safeguard *decent* values. The catastrophic outcome of this complacency was that my family, six million Jews and countless other minorities were gassed, brutalised and enslaved.

My grandfather never told me his story in one sitting. It existed in whispers of '*what he'd been through*' that would follow eccentric behaviour, or appeared in food wrapped in napkins stored at the back of cupboards (just in case) or in the unspoken-of scars on his face and back. It came in sudden outbursts like parts of a missing jigsaw.

Yet I never saw him - despite everything - express a word of hate towards his tormentors. The opposite. He believed in the fundamental truth that all of us - from every background and community - have within us the courage to stand up to tyranny and prejudice.

To have heard his account and those of other survivors is to be forever changed. I have listened to these stories many times. They are threads that have woven themselves into my tapestry and those of countless others. We are all witnesses and custodians of truth, imbued with a purpose expressed so beautifully at the heart of an ancient Jewish prayer called *the Shema* that I recall my grandfather reciting and were the last words on the lips of millions of the Nazi's victims; "*You shall teach your children.*"

Sadly my grandfather passed away two decades ago and the number of survivors is quickly diminishing. But the power of their stories to shape the lives of our children; to gift them the determination to be a light in the world is limitless. I often think of the first question children ask the survivors; "*Why don't you hate?*" The answer given is nearly always the same: "*What good would that do, the world needs to hear us so that people can learn.*"

Joel Stern's book 'Just Freddy' is a personal testimony. The story is his family's. It is written from a child's perspective with the mission of all the survivors at its core; that we should teach our children so we might finally learn that message from over a century ago; that the world must never forget the past or we are doomed to repeat it.

The book also reminds us all that, despite the seemingly endless cycle of horror, we must never surrender our optimism, our shared innate gift for love, compassion and tolerance towards each other as this is the light within every person. It is the most powerful weapon we share against hate and despair.

But this light needs to be rekindled, renewed and taught to each generation or the forces of darkness will continue to shape and dominate our world.

1. BIRTHDAY
JUNE 1937

Dlang...

Dlang...

Dlang...

The sound of the school bell signalled the end of the day. The three boys quickly gathered up their books into their leather satchels and made for the cluster of students at the door who were waiting their turn to pour out of the classroom. They shuffled along the corridor, being almost carried along towards the main entrance. The atrium was dark and cool but filled with the noise of excited children, the summer heat beaming in the doorway, drawing them out into the warmth and brightness of a beautiful afternoon in the German Westerwald.

It was June 9th, and Freddy Stern was celebrating his twelfth birthday. Together with his best friends Josef Zimmermann and Adolf Vögel, they ran through the gothic market town of Montabaur, their satchels flying behind them. They knew this route well, undertaking it back and forth each day. They passed Fleishmann's butcher shop that flaunted an array of sausages of all shapes and sizes in the window. The incredible smell wafting out of Luftmann's bakery drifted with them for a number of paces as they

5

ran past, and remained in their nostrils for some time more. The large red brick town hall, looming over the cobbled central square, kept guard over its citizens passing below as they went about their daily lives. The boys darted past Herr Motzi, the local beggar who was known to everyone, jangling his tin cup of small coins without even an acknowledgement. They rounded the corner into Bahnhofstrasse, where, about one hundred yards in front of them, was the grey three-storey home of Freddy and his parents, Meyer and Betty.

At the front of the house was Meyer's leather workshop. The store had a large, open frontage, above which stood a sign painted with black script lettering on a white, now yellowing board reading "Alexander Stern – Leather Craft since 1876". With Freddy leading the pack, the boys ran in through the front of the store, straight past the large, wooden tanning vats, the hanging animal hides and Freddy's father, who was hammering away at a skin with a large metal mallet. They reached the steep stairs at the back of the house and ascended into the flat above where Freddy and his family lived.

The boys arrived into a roomy, open hallway where they were greeted by Freddy's mother, who couldn't contain the huge grin on her face.

"Welcome home, sweet birthday boy," she said as Freddy grimaced with embarrassment. "Drop your bags there," she told Zimmermann and Vögel, pointing to a large trunk, above which hung coats, jackets and a black, wide brimmed fedora hat, "and then come on through." Her voice echoed back into the hallway as she disappeared through one of the large doorways into the kitchen.

On the table lay three plates, together with an assortment of sandwiches, pretzel sticks and caramelised nuts, but the boys' attention was immediately drawn to a jug of cold lemon juice, condensation dripping down its side. Betty poured three cups out, and the boys gulped down the satisfyingly sweet freshness, quenching their thirst and cooling the sweat they had picked up running through town on such a warm day. She refilled their glasses and offered round some sandwiches.

"Don't you have liver sausage?" asked Zimmermann. "That's my favourite!"

"I'm sorry," replied Freddy's mother, "but we don't eat liver sausage in our house. We're Jewish, and we keep kosher."

By now, Freddy's father had joined the group in the kitchen. He had come up from his workshop and was washing his hands in the sink.

"What is Jewish?" asked Zimmermann.

"Well," replied Betty, looking across the kitchen at her husband, "it means that we have the same God as Christians, but we worship him in a different way. We celebrate the sabbath on a Saturday instead of a Sunday, and we pray in a synagogue instead of a church. There are certain foods we're forbidden from eating, like pork and salami, but there are other foods we make and eat that are also very delicious. Apart from that, we're no different from any other Germans."

"I still like liver sausage." said Zimmermann, taking a bite out of his cheese sandwich.

"Of course you do!" replied Vögel, raising his eyebrows, and the three boys burst into laughter.

"Ok, Freddy, close your eyes," said Betty and as he did, she uncovered a huge apple streusel on the counter. The masterpiece, a large, moist, fluffy muffin-type cake, was baked with apples from Freddy's grandparents' garden in the nearby town of Herborn, which they had harvested on a visit just a few weeks earlier. On top of the streusel was a light, crumbly topping made of flour, butter and sugar, cooked until golden and giving off the most incredible fragrance. It was Freddy's favourite, and as his friends began to sing "Happy Birthday," he opened his eyes, saw the streusel in front of him and was unable to hide his joy. Surrounded by his parents, best friends and the biggest streusel he'd ever seen, Freddy would have happily admitted that life couldn't get much better!

A few hours later, once his friends had filled their bellies and headed home, Freddy's father went to his son, cocked his neck as if to tell Freddy to follow and headed back down the steep staircase to his workshop, through a narrow, damp corridor and out through a door into the family's back garden. There, beneath the loving gaze of his mother, who was looking down on the pair from an upstairs window, Meyer took Freddy to the side of a small shed they had in the garden and lifted up a blanket, under which stood a brand new Dürkopp bicycle. His family were not wealthy, and with many cousins living very close by, Freddy had never had anything brand new before. He stood in wonderment, staring at the shiny, red, wide-wheeled bike, unable to speak. He threw his arms around his father, who returned the embrace, wrapping Freddy up in his large, muscular arms, and the two of them stayed there, locked together, for what seemed like hours.

The following day was Saturday, the Jewish sabbath. As she did each week, Freddy's mother had laid out his good clothes on the chair in his bedroom for him, ready for when he got up. Even though they weren't very religious, every Saturday morning, the family put on their finery and walked the short distance down Bahnhofstrasse, turning left onto Judengasse (Jew Lane), which was named after the first Jews of Montabaur, who had lived on that street, and continued towards the synagogue. It took no more than five minutes, and often, they bumped into Freddy's paternal cousins, Rudi, a rambunctious boy the same age as Freddy, and his younger sister Gabsy, on the way there. Freddy found the synagogue service a bore and detested being made to sit still in his scratchy, smart clothes on the hard wooden pews which made his backside go to sleep. The boredom of the service was somewhat helped by the company of Rudi. The two boys would make sure they were sitting together and would spend much of the three hours of the service whispering to each other, telling jokes, or discussing school gossip, while constantly being told to quiet down by their fathers. Often, they would challenge each other to wrap the strings of their fathers' tallits, Jewish prayer shawls, so tightly around their fingers until they turned blue, just to see which of them could achieve the bluest finger.

But this Saturday was different. Freddy didn't want to go to synagogue. He wanted to take his new Dürkopp bike out into the countryside, explore the local paths and trails and enjoy his new-found freedom. He had ignored the clothes laid out by his mother, instead dressing in leather shorts and a short-sleeved shirt, but had been sent back to his room by his father to change before being allowed any breakfast. Freddy had begged his parents for just one week's exception from the sabbath morning service, but they were having none of it. Instead, he had been told that if he didn't get changed and get ready to go to synagogue, he wouldn't be allowed out in the afternoon either. Begrudgingly, Freddy got dressed into the clothes he loathed, wolfed down a slice of bread and butter and headed down the stairs to the street with his parents, still pulling at his shirt collar to try and stop it itching.

The service that Saturday was the worst Freddy could remember. It felt less like the traditional sabbath morning service and more like the annual Day of Atonement, when they weren't allowed to eat or drink and had to spend *all day* in the synagogue. The three hours felt like twelve as Freddy and Rudi excitedly whispered their plans for the afternoon to each other, receiving constant shushes and tuts from the other members of the congregation. They had planned to set out north from the town, heading towards the village of Meudt, where Freddy's father had been born and where they could stop at the village café for a rest and a glass of lemon juice before heading back through the shady forest of the Westerwald. Just as they had decided on their route for the afternoon, they were hit with a particularly loud "sshhhh" from a few rows behind them. As the boys quietened and tuned into Rabbi Zeitlin, who was delivering his sermon from the pulpit, Freddy noticed a strange air of silence that wasn't usually present.

Ordinarily, during the sermon, he'd hear the whispering of children (and some adults), the rustling of toffee wrappers, even an occasional snore. But this week, deafening silence reigned as everyone seemed to be giving their full attention to the Rabbi. Even the sounds of the bustling market in the next street seemed to quieten and, in the eerie silence of the sanctuary, Freddy heard a word he had never heard before: Hitler.

2. HITLER
MARCH 1938

The sun rose over the top of the hill at the back of the house, streaming in through Freddy's bedroom window, bringing light and warmth into the room. The boy stirred but quickly dozed off again before a loud knock on the door brought him to. He dragged himself out of bed, washed, dressed and wandered, still half asleep, into the kitchen, where his mother had prepared a boiled egg with toast soldiers.

"I'm going shopping this morning," she told him. "So I can walk you to school." Freddy winced, wrinkling his nose up and making a huffing noise. He disliked his mother taking him to school, and had been walking himself and meeting his friends on the way for over two years, but he knew she had enjoyed their morning walks in the past and he didn't have the heart to say that he wanted to go by himself.

"Ok," he said, barely looking up at her, "I'll get my bag and shoes."

Waving goodbye to his dad, who had already been working for a number of hours after receiving an early morning delivery of cow hides, they left the workshop and turned left towards town. As they walked towards the town square, they felt an unusual buzz of excitement. There were lots of people already out and about at this early hour, many more than usual, and everyone seemed to be either chatting, smiling or laughing. As they turned the corner into the square Freddy and his mother saw the reason for the eagerness of their fellow townsfolk.

Overnight, the town hall had been adorned in huge, red banners hanging down from the upper windows and there was a new flag positioned above the door. In the middle of the banners was a large, white circle with a black cross inside it. Freddy felt his mother grip his hand more tightly and her pace quicken as they walked past.

"Mum, what are those?" he asked her.

"Swastikas." she replied curtly. "The symbol of the Nazi Party. Just ignore them."

And off to school they went.

At breaktime, Freddy assembled in the schoolyard with Zimmermann and Vögel, as they always did. It was a particularly cold spring day, and the boys were dressed in woollen hats and scarves, hopping from foot to foot to try and keep warm as they decided what to play.

"How about Soldiers?" suggested Vögel. Freddy liked playing soldiers. He had always admired his father's collection of medals from the Great War, which hung in a frame in their hallway, and Freddy had always felt a great sense of pride as he walked past these mementoes honouring his family's contribution to German history. He also loved the bedtime stories his father told him about his experiences during the war, such as when they ran out of food and had to catch wild pheasants to eat or the time he just managed to escape being blown up by an English bomb because he had an upset stomach and had been on the toilet when his post had been hit.

Without waiting for a definitive answer from his friends, Vögel added, "But I should be Adolf Hitler, seeing as my name is Adolf, too. That means I'm the Führer, and you guys need to follow my command, ok?"

Freddy and Zimmermann both raised their eyebrows at each other but nodded and proceeded to take orders from Vögel. The boys cocked their arms at shoulder height, as if holding rifles, although at times, Freddy preferred to lower his arms as if he were holding a machine gun. This always brought disparagement from Vögel because infantry soldiers wouldn't have machine guns and it made it too easy, but both Freddy and Zimmermann took great pleasure in using this ploy to wind Vögel up.

"What are you losers doing?"

The sneering question came from Horst Fuchs, a blonde and well-toned boy, who, despite being the same age as Freddy and his friends, had been moved up a year because of his intelligence and, for some reason, always seemed much bigger physically, too. Fuchs stood in front of the boys, his hands on his hips and wearing a smart uniform of dark brown leather trousers with a lighter brown shirt tucked into a large, silver belt buckle around his waist and a khaki green neckerchief around his neck. There was a red band around his left arm with a swastika on it, like the one Freddy had seen draped on the town hall that morning. Attached to his belt was a holster, holding a small hunting knife with a shiny brass handle. Freddy had never seen such a smart uniform before. It looked a bit like what he wore for scouts, but at scouts, they had horrible, grey shorts, with no belt and which kept falling down, and they certainly weren't allowed to carry knives around with them.

"We're playing Soldiers." said Vögel, looking admiringly at Fuchs.

"You're playing Soldiers … with *him*?" Fuchs said, directing his gaze straight at Freddy.

Freddy didn't know how to respond. He had never liked Horst Fuchs, but for the most part, since Fuchs had been moved up a year, they hadn't had much to do with each other. Freddy had always tried to steer out of his way, knowing that Fuchs liked to bully pupils who were smaller than himself, but he had never had a confrontation like this with him before.

"We always play Soldiers together," replied Freddy.

"But *you're* a Jew!" came Fuchs' response, shrill and biting. "Jews can't fight, they're inferior," he continued.

"Oh, get lost Fuchs," said Zimmermann, taking a step

towards the larger boy. Josef Zimmermann had always tried to stay out of trouble, preferring to run away from confrontation rather than embrace it. However, on this occasion, he had come to the defence of his best friend without even thinking. It was a purely instinctive reaction. And now, looking at Fuch's face, he was starting to regret it.

Fuchs also took a step forwards, but towards Freddy rather than Zimmermann, coming inches away and towering at least half a foot over him. He scrunched his face up, drew his eyes into narrow slits and stared at him, unflinchingly.

Then, he burst out laughing, cackling in a grim tone. "You'll see. You'll see what's coming to you, *Jew*," he muttered through the laughter as he turned away and walked back to re-join his friends on the other side of the playground.

After the confrontation with Fuchs, none of the boys felt like playing Soldiers anymore. Instead, they spoke quietly about the lessons they had coming up that afternoon and how Freddy had had a lucky escape earlier when Herr Richter, their maths teacher, had singled him out in class to answer a particularly tricky sum.

In between chatter about maths and German history, Vögel asked, "Did you see what Fuchs was wearing? That Hitler Youth uniform is so cool. My dad said I can go to Hitler Youth camp this summer. I hope they give me clothes like that. And did you *see* the hunting knife?"

"Yeah, I'd quite like to go to camp, too," said Zimmermann. "I've heard it's really fun, building dens, foraging for food, hunting and making campfires. I just hope Fuchs isn't there. I hate that kid. He's just so mean for no reason."

Freddy stayed silent. The idea of camp really excited him, and he loved exploring the countryside around Montabaur, but the idea of spending the summer holidays in close proximity to Horst Fuchs made him question whether it would be a smart idea.

After school, as he often did, Freddy walked in through the front door of his father's workshop, dropped his schoolbag and coat at the bottom of the staircase leading up to the family's flat and then returned into the workshop and pulled himself up so that he was sitting on the workbench where his father was working. Freddy could sit and watch his dad work for hours. He loved how such a strong and powerful man was able to manage the heavy lifting of the animal hides but also work so delicately and intricately, producing highly skilled leather items such as wallets and purses. The satchel that Freddy took to school each day had been made by his father, a unique piece with Freddy's initials stitched into the dark brown leather with a golden yellow thread.

Meyer Stern was a large man, over six feet tall and with broad shoulders. His muscular arms had been developed over many years, moving the heavy hides and barrels of tannin around in his workshop. He wore a thin moustache that transformed the rugged craftsman into a more sophisticated picture when he was away from work. He was president of the local gymnastics association and often spent evenings and weekends at the gymnastics club in the town, exercising in the gym, developing his physique and ensuring that he was in top health to be able to carry out his work and keep providing for his family. Around town, Meyer was known as a reputable businessman, a hard worker and was both respected and appreciated for his efforts in aiding the community through his work with the gymnastics club. He would often host gymnasts from other towns at their home when they were in town to compete in tournaments, and had spent a lot of time helping younger members of the club develop their skills. Freddy, though, had never shown any kind of natural aptitude for sport, he was far too skinny, scrawny and weak, not to mention that he had little interest in sports.

Freddy's relationship with his father was mostly good, though he found that his dad could become easily stressed, and Freddy's love for playing practical jokes did nothing to help that. Mostly, the victim of his pranks was his cousin, Gabsy, who was a few years younger than Freddy and very innocent and naïve. However, one time, while his father had been away for the weekend with the gymnastics club, Freddy had found himself with nothing to do. His mother was busy in the kitchen, and his cousins weren't available to play. Freddy had wandered down to Meyer's workshop and spotted the typewriter sitting on the desk in the office, which his father used to type letters to customers and suppliers and prepare his orders and invoices requesting payments. Although he wasn't interested in sports, Freddy had a love for mechanics and understanding how things worked, and he spent two hours taking the typewriter to pieces before switching the letters on the typebars around. After putting it all back together, he still had a few screws to spare, but was sure it could pass, and it did. After his father returned from his trip on Sunday evening, he headed down to his office to prepare his orders for the following morning. As he tried to type, he couldn't work out why every letter he typed produced an incorrectly corresponding letter on his paper. It didn't take too long for him to realise who was responsible, and when he did, Freddy was unable to sit down comfortably for three days. After spending half the night attempting to put the typewriter back together, Meyer had had to call an engineer to come and repair it properly.

After silently watching his father work for a while, Meyer looked up and saw his son. He took him in; the baby boy he had been so proud to hold and show off to his friends in the gymnastics club and the synagogue was now a tall, scrawny, but slender and handsome young man, growing up faster than he dared to think about.

"Come on, get your bike," said Meyer. "I'm sure Frau Kahn won't mind waiting an extra day to get her bag repaired." He winked at his son as he wiped his hands on his apron and stood up from the workbench.

That evening, as the family were sitting around the table eating their evening meal, Betty asked her son about his day at school.

"Hmm, it was ok," replied Freddy. "Herr Richter was in a bad mood again, and at breaktime, I played with Zimmermann and Vögel." His mother smiled as she watched Freddy shovelling meatloaf into his mouth as if he hadn't eaten for days. Through his mouthfuls, Freddy asked, "Can I go to Hitler Youth camp in the summer?"

Meyer dropped his cutlery onto his plate. Freddy stopped eating and looked up at his dad who was shaking, beads of sweat began to appear on his forehead.

"No," replied Meyer, sharply.

"But Dad, Vögel and Zimmermann are going, and I don't want to be the only one…"

"I said no."

"But Dad …"

That was it. He had gone too far.

Meyer stood up quickly, and before Freddy knew what was happening, his father grabbed his ear and dragged him out of his seat and out of the dining room. His father was pulling so hard on his ear that Freddy thought he might actually pull it off.

"Ow, Ow, Ow, Dad, Ow!" screamed Freddy as Meyer, still holding tight to his ear, dragged him down the corridor and pushed him into his bedroom.

"No means no!" Meyer said slowly and coldly through his now heavy breaths, slamming the bedroom door shut as Freddy ran onto his bed and buried his head into his pillow.

Freddy sobbed and sobbed. He couldn't understand why an innocent request such as going to summer camp had provoked such a stern reaction from his father. His pillow was now wet, dampened by his tears, and his ear still throbbed from the assault. It was at least an hour before there was a light knock and his bedroom door opened gently. Standing there, silhouetted against the light in the hallway, was his mother with a plate of food.

"I brought you the rest of your supper and a piece of cake for desert," she said gently, inviting herself into his dark bedroom. She placed the plate of food on top of the wooden chest of drawers and moved to sit down on the edge of his bed. The gross upset and injustice Freddy was feeling was clear for her to see and she put her hand onto his face, cradling his cheek while rubbing away his tears with her thumb.

"I don't understand Mum," sobbed Freddy. "I only asked if I could go to camp. I didn't mean to disrespect Dad."

"I know, I know. But, Freddy, your father is just trying to protect you. You might not understand this now, but one day, you will. It's just his way. He loves you more than you can know, and he only wants what is best for you."

"But Mum, why doesn't Dad want me to go to summer camp?"

"Because," Betty replied, "those camps are only for German children. They don't let others go."

"But I *am* German," said Freddy, brow furrowed.

"Yes, but you are also Jewish. These camps are for German *Christian* children," she said.

Betty could sense her son's bewilderment and couldn't think how to explain it better. "But don't worry," she added, "you can still do fun things in the summer; perhaps, you can go camping with Rudi and Gabsy in Herborn?"

Freddy looked at her and nodded, showing he understood that he needed to let this one go. Betty stood up and walked back towards the door, turning to look at her son before shuffling out. A tear ran down her cheek as she closed the door, leaving it slightly ajar so that a strip of light could provide Freddy with some illumination as he began to nibble at his supper.

3. DEPARTURES
AUGUST 1938

Time seemed to have slowed down, and every day felt like a week, every week a month. For ages, they had been planning their camping trip. Vögel and Zimmermann had already left for summer camp, a full six weeks away in the countryside, and although Freddy and his cousins only had a week for their trip, Freddy could not contain his excitement. He and Rudi had made a packing list and devised a number of pranks they planned to play on Gabsy.

Finally, the day arrived. Freddy had packed everything into a large duffel bag which he could barely lift. He had made his way down the packing list, ensuring that each and every item he and Rudi had noted was included and stashed away. Meyer carried the bag down the steep staircase from the apartment into the workshop, followed by Freddy, with his mother behind them. At the shop entrance, his father handed over the bag, which Freddy managed to heave onto his shoulder before giving his dad a hug.

"Be good," Meyer said, "and say hello to your grandparents."

"I will, Dad," replied Freddy and with that, he turned away and walked out of the shop with his mother.

They walked down the street together, Freddy unable to keep quiet, telling his mother all about the plans he had for his week away. After about one hundred yards, they came to Uncle

Ernest and Aunt Margaret's house, and as Freddy tried to bound up the five concrete steps to the front door, he almost tumbled down under the weight of his bag. He made it to the top and banged on the door; it didn't take long for the ruddy-faced Rudi to appear, a huge grin on his face.

Trailed by Gabsy and their mothers, the boys made it to the train station at the bottom of Bahnhofstrasse, and when the 11:05 arrived, they boarded, found their compartment and pulled down the windows to say goodbye to their mothers. This was the first time Freddy had been away by himself without either of his parents, and as the train began to pull slowly out of Montabaur station, Betty felt a faint but distinct sense of loss. Her son was growing up, beginning to make a visible transition from child to adult. He'd become so independent.

It was a slow two-hour ride from Montabaur, through the Westerwald to the town of Herborn. Although the journey was relatively short, their mothers had furnished them with all sorts of delicious food for their picnic, and as soon as the train had pulled out of the station, they were already unwrapping sandwiches, herring rollmops, biscuits and cakes. Freddy even had a small square of chocolate. The food didn't last long, and so, to dull the boredom that would otherwise have followed, Freddy and Rudi began their schedule of practical jokes on Gabsy.

"Hey, Gabs," said Rudi, "I bet you couldn't fit on the

luggage rack up there!" he said, gesturing with his head towards the metal-rimmed, netted shelf, high on the wall above little Gabsy.

"I bet I could!" she replied defiantly.

"Prove it then," said Freddy, "We'll help you up!".

Having been so defiant, Gabsy had no choice but to comply, and as the two boys gave her a leg-up, she hauled herself onto the rack, laying on it with her knees up to her chest.

"See, I told you I could fit! Now, help me down"

"Hmm…" mused Rudi, stroking his chin.

"Come on! Help me down!" shouted Gabsy, "I'm starting to feel sick."

"Na!" chimed Freddy and Rudi in unison, as Gabsy's protests landed on deaf ears whilst the boys rolled around on their seats in fits of laughter. It didn't take long for Freddy and Rudi to get bored of Gabsy's whinging and they eventually helped her down. Without saying a word, she slapped Rudi around the head and then placed herself on the seat next to the window, staring out without acknowledging her tormentors so they knew she was upset with them. Whilst Freddy knew that singling out Gabsy like this was slightly mean, the fact she mostly took it in good humour and came around *eventually*, made him think that she secretly liked the attention of the older boys.

The countryside they were travelling through was familiar

to them, and they had often enjoyed trips, both with each other's families and separately with their own parents out of the town. Freddy, especially, was well versed on the journey to Herborn, where his grandparents lived. As the train pulled into Herborn station, the three children had already found their way to the carriage door and had pulled down the window, ready to open it. Freddy immediately recognised the short, white-haired man with the wide moustache as his grandfather, shouting "Papa David!" from the window and waving frantically as the train moved slowly past him. Before it had even stopped, Freddy had opened the door and thrown his bag off before jumping down himself and running back along the platform to embrace his grandfather.

David Lowenstein was Freddy's maternal grandfather and the member of the family to whom Freddy felt closest. He was a cattle dealer, breeding, raising, selling and trading cows and supplying, among others, Freddy's father with skins for his leather business. David and his wife, Rosa, lived on the edge of the town of Herborn in a farmhouse with land backing onto the river Dill. Some of Freddy's happiest childhood memories had been at his grandparent's home, helping his grandfather with the cows, picking fruit from the trees in their orchard and swimming in the river. He had spent many of his school holidays there with his mother, and there never seemed to be a boring moment when he visited his grandparents. Despite being well into his sixties and still working long days on the cattle farm, Papa David always found time to spend with his grandson when he came to visit and loved to show him how things worked. As his only grandchild, Freddy's visits were an excuse for Papa David to revert into more childish ways, and the two of them were often scorned by Grandma Rosa for being as thick as thieves and getting into mischief. Grandma Rosa, on the other hand, was a short and dour woman, almost as wide as she was tall. She also helped out on the farm and was as strong as she was stubborn. She made a mean strudel and, just like her daughter Betty, took great delight in feeding up her grandson.

"You're too thin! Do they not feed you in Montabaur? She would always say.

There was another person who lived with his grandparents, Freddy's aunt, Herta. His mother's younger sister was thirty-two, unmarried and worked as a saleswoman in a clothing shop for rich ladies in the town. She took great pride in her appearance, making sure she was dressed at the height of modern fashion and was embarrassed by her humble farming background and the way that her parents dressed in worker's clothing on their farm. She was an attractive lady who had many boyfriends but could never make up her mind about any of them, always looking for perfection. Herta was a complex person, cold in demeanour with a tall and slender frame, completely unlike either of her parents. She despised Freddy and hated his visits because it meant that all her parent's attention was diverted to her nephew. Every time she caught her father staring lovingly at his grandson, or her mother giving Freddy a second helping of desert without him even asking, the jealously inside Herta rose, driving her irrational and unfair dislike for him. For his part, Freddy knew how Aunt Herta felt about him and tried to stay out of her way as much as possible. Even *he* wouldn't be crazy enough to dare to play a prank on Aunt Herta!

The boys loaded their bags onto the back of the cart and then jumped on themselves while Papa David carried Gabsy's bag, before lifting her into the front. He untied Prinz the horse from the hitching post and then jumped up onto the front of the cart, alongside Gabsy. As they trotted through town, with the hot afternoon sun burning down on them, Freddy took great delight in pointing out some of the local sights to his cousins. Eventually, they arrived at the farm, and as his grandfather brought Prinz to a stop and hopped down from the cart to tie him, Freddy saw his grandmother come out from the farmhouse to greet them. She was larger than he remembered, or perhaps she'd just put on extra weight since his last visit at Easter. Behind her, with a miserable look on her face and her arms crossed, stood Aunt Herta, leaning against the doorway.

"Watch out for her," Freddy muttered to Rudi while waving hello to his Aunt, "and whatever you do, don't upset her!"

The children jumped down from the cart and were ushered into the parlour where Grandma Rosa presented them with sandwiches and cake, which, despite having already had ample to eat on the train, the boys took great delight in tucking into. Grandma Rosa looked on while Papa David sat at the table with the children and asked them questions about the journey, school and their lives back in Montabaur.

"Well," began Freddy, "all my friends went to Hitler Youth camp and I really wanted to go but Dad wouldn't let me ..."

His grandfather nodded. "Yes, I understand. But we're going to have a great week here. Better than any Hitler Youth camp!" He tousled Freddy's hair before popping a piece of cake into his mouth.

After eating, Papa David, Freddy, Rudi and Gabsy headed back out to where Prinz was tethered, and with the children back on board, Papa David led the dappled horse up through the farm and down a dirt track towards the back of the property. They passed by paddocks with large brown and white cows eating from grain barrels below, through the orchard with its apple, pear and plum trees and down through a small meadow towards the riverbank where they would make camp. Papa David helped unload the cart while Gabsy took off her shoes and dipped her toes in the river Dill. The boys set to work erecting their tent, and once it was pegged out, they lit a small campfire. Papa David gave the children a small bag of potatoes and some butter from the farm and then bade farewell, returning back to the farmhouse with Prinz. It was around 7 p. m., and the temperature was beginning to drop. Rudi placed the potatoes into the embers to cook, and the three children sat around the fire, waiting for their meal to be ready while inhaling the mesmerising scent of the burning pine logs on the fire.

It was still dark outside when Rudi reached over and shook Freddy awake.

"Fred … shhh … listen," he said, holding his index finger against his lips.

Freddy woke with a start and listened intently. Sure enough, it sounded like there was somebody outside. They could hear whomever it was moving around the camp, but it soon became clear that it wasn't a person, but an animal.

"Are there wolves in Herborn?" Rudi whispered to his cousin. Freddy shrugged and furrowed his brow. He'd never seen a wolf while visiting his grandparents or heard them talk of one, but that didn't mean they weren't there.

"Perhaps one of Papa's cows has escaped?" he replied, thinking that a cow would be less of a danger than a wolf. Whatever it was, it was now right up against the tent and, silhouetted against the light of the bright moon, it looked big! Gabsy slept soundly and the two boys stared silently, watching the side of the tent move as the animal rustled up against it. And then, as quickly as it had come, it was gone. Whatever it was, had left, and the boys, stirred by the adrenalin of both fear and excitement, lay awake, watching the roof of their tent as the light outside brightened from deep blacks into a full, bright dawn.

It was a very hot day and unusually humid for the

Westerwald. Still tired from their journey and the early start, the children decided to stay close to camp for the day and enjoy the cool river. After he had finished his morning work, Papa David arrived with Prinz, bringing some supplies, including fresh plum juice, bread, eggs and some beef sausages. Papa David asked how they had slept, and as Freddy was about to tell him about their late night visitor, he felt a sharp jab in his ribs from Rudi and decided that perhaps it wasn't the best idea to disclose this to his grandfather. Assured that the children were all ok, Papa David returned to his farm, and the children spent time exploring the area around their camp, fishing and swimming in the river. As they were swimming, the boys took great pleasure in spontaneously shouting "Crocodile! Crocodile!" They knew full well that there were no crocodiles in Germany, but Gabsy didn't and it was hilarious to watch her reaction as she screamed and ran for the bank.

In the evening, Freddy proudly pulled out a grill he had brought with him. He had found it on the street in Montabaur, put out with someone's trash and had spent hours painstakingly restoring and cleaning it up so that it looked almost as good as new. The boys set the fire while Gabsy gathered more wood from the forested area close to camp. Once it was hot enough, they set the grill over the fire and took out the sausages Papa David had brought in the morning, which had been kept cool in a tributary channel of the river. Freddy used a machete he had brought from his father's shed to whittle down a stick into a point and used it to turn the sausages until they browned. Once the sausages were ready, Freddy and Rudi worked together using sticks to remove the grill from the fire so that the sausages wouldn't burn, then, they all dived in, enjoying their self-cooked meal.

Just then, there was a rustling in the bushes close to the river, around twenty feet away. They all heard it and turned to see.

"I saw something move!" said Rudi.

"I'm not falling for this again," Said Gabsy, "you've done this prank already!

"No, really, I did!"

"Yeah, yeah, whatever!" came her sarcastic reply.

The rustling noise came again and this time, Gabsy took a few steps back, away from where the bushes were.

"Stop it!" said Gabsy. "Whatever you've done, it's not funny!"

Suddenly, a small black object darted out in a blur, heading for the camp. It was only when it got really close, they realised it was a dog. Before they knew it, the hound was on them and was devouring the remaining sausages from the grill. Freddy and Rudi looked at each other, relief on their faces but then quickly realised that the young terrier was eating their supper.

Freddy got up and went over to the dog, leaning down to pick it up, sausage still in its mouth. He held the bedraggled animal out in front of him, staring into its eyes, and smiled at it.

"Hello Mr Trouble!" said Freddy. "Where did you come from?"

"It doesn't look like he's been well looked after," Gabsy said. "And look how hungry he is."

"He must be a stray," said Rudi.

"Well, if he's going to be hanging around with us, we should give him a name." Freddy said. "Look at this ginger hair around his mouth. He looks like old Herr Landau from the synagogue with his big ginger moustache. Let's call him Landau."

The next few days were spent having a great time; exploring the countryside and the farm, helping Papa David with the cows and taking Prinz out with the cart for rides around the town, all with Landau in tow. Freddy had never enjoyed a summer vacation so much and had become inseparable from the dog. Likewise, Landau had developed a love for his new human friend. Wherever Freddy went, Landau would follow, and even when they slept in the tent at night, Landau would curl up next to Freddy, who in turn, would envelop the small dog with his body.

One evening, as the children walked back down the path from the farm to their camp after supper, Landau following behind them, Freddy's thoughts began to turn to the end of their trip in a few days and a return to their parents in Montabaur.

"I wonder if we can take Landau back with us?" Freddy asked.

"Yes!" Gabsy said. "He can come and live with us. He can sleep in the small shed next to the grain store in our yard."

"Don't be silly," replied Rudi to his sister. "Of course he can't come and stay with us. Who will look after him when we move to London?"

"Who's moving to London?" asked Freddy.

"You weren't meant to say anything!" Gabsy scolded her older brother, shooting him a look.

"Yeah, mum and dad said that we have to move to London because Germany isn't safe for Jews anymore. We're going at the end of the summer so that we can settle in before the new school year begins," Rudi said, more quietly now, trying not to catch Freddy's eye.

Unsure what to say or how to respond, all Freddy could think to say was, "But you don't speak English?"

Gabsy replied, "We can learn it. Father has arranged for us to start in a school with other Jewish immigrants, so there will be some other Germans there with us."

They continued back to camp in silence, and when they

arrived, Freddy sat on a log beside the ashen remains of their campfire, looking into the thick summer dusk air ahead of him. Sensing something wasn't right in the way that dogs do, Landau bounded up to him and began to lick his face, which brought out a smile even though, deep down inside, he was crushed, and struggling to hold back his tears.

Rudi and Gabsy were his cousins, but they spent so much time together, that without any siblings of his own, they felt more like a brother and sister to him. The smallest, most ridiculous thoughts were bothering Freddy. How would Gabsy, so diminutive in stature, manage to jump on to the high-back entrance of a London bus? Where would Rudi get his favourite Lebkuchen biscuits from at Christmas time? Would Uncle Ernest have the same job in London, or would he have to find a new one? Such simple things, such ridiculous things to think about, but it was the only way he could think to deal with the news.

Freddy had told Rudi every secret he ever had. Who would he have to confide in once Rudi was gone? And Gabsy, little Gabsy who was so often the butt of their jokes; did she know just how deeply he cared for her and how much he admired her tenacity to put up with everything the boys threw at her? Just then, Landau caught his eye, and Freddy knew that he would have to take the dog home with him. Otherwise, he would have nobody.

4. NOTES
NOVEMBER 1938

Summer seemed to transition into autumn very quickly that year Freddy thought, as he gazed out the classroom window, watching the russet leaves falling from the large trees in the playground, whirling around in a strange kind of dance against the backdrop of the dark grey morning sky. Behind the twirling leaves, he could make out the yellow-painted turret of Montabaur Castle, sitting proudly at the top of the hill, a focal point of the town. The yellow-painted exterior seemed darker than he remembered, and he drifted into a memory of the previous spring, when he and Rudi had dared Gabsy to try and run down the hill. She had slipped and gone into a head-over-heel tumble, rolling down the steep slope until she came to a stop up against a large tree with a bump. He remembered how they had laughed so hard at the time but that the beating he had received from his father as a result had left his backside as red a tomato.

"Stern!" bellowed Herr Richter, snapping Freddy out of his daydream.

Maths was Freddy's least favourite subject, mostly because his teacher, Herr Richter, was renowned for using a birch branch that he kept on the chalk shelf under the blackboard for scolding pupils who were unable to correctly answer his questions.

"Yes, Herr Richter," replied Freddy.

"What is 8 multiplied by 12?"

Freddy hesitated, trying to arrive at the answer quickly, but knowing that it had to be right, otherwise, he would likely face the birch branch. But he didn't have time to work it out, he had already been caught daydreaming. He had to deliver an answer. *Now!*

"Erm … 96 sir?" he replied, with a distinct sound of uncertainty in his voice.

"Correct," said Herr Richter, a tone of slight disappointment slipping in, "… but you took too long. Put out your hand." He reached for the birch branch.

Panic set in. What on earth was going on? A caning for a wrong answer, yes, sure, but he'd never known Herr Richter to dish one out for a correct answer. The wiry teacher strode up the aisle of desks as the other children looked on in concerned bewilderment. This was a new phenomenon for them, too. It was almost like Herr Richter was punishing Freddy for some other reason. Freddy had taken a couple of canings before, and although there was always an initial flash of pain and heat, it had always subsided quite quickly, and the longer-term effects were minimal. But this time, Herr Richter looked like a man on a mission. Freddy held out his hand, knowing that arguing would only make it worse, trying to stop himself from trembling as Herr Richter lifted the dreaded birch. The classroom door swung open, and Herr Bayer, the headmaster, stood there with his arms crossed.

"Herr Richter," he said calmly, "I need to see Stern in my office immediately."

And with that, he turned on his heel and walked out. Herr Richter lowered the birch.

"You heard Herr Bayer," he barked, gazing through Freddy with a look of icy coldness. "Immediately!"

Freddy stood, gathered his books into his satchel and went to leave the classroom, almost at a jog.

What could Herr Bayer possibly want to see me about? He'd been especially careful not to play any pranks at school this year after a very severe talking to from his father on the eve of the new term, and his grades weren't *that* bad. He had never been called to see the headmaster before and had absolutely no idea if it would be better or worse than a caning from Herr Richter.

The walk down the corridor from the classroom seemed to go on and on. At the end of the hallway, Freddy climbed the stone staircase up to the first floor, at the top of which was a large wooden door with a sign that read, "Herr. M. Bayer. Headmaster." Freddy knocked on the door.

"Come in," replied the man on the other side.

Freddy opened the door and saw that Herr Bayer's office was big, almost double the size of Freddy's classroom. Against the left-hand wall were shelves holding hundreds of different books, which all looked very important. Freddy could see encyclopaedias and history books, among all types of books, big and small filling every shelf from floor to ceiling. Against the right-hand wall was a large painting, a portrait of a man Freddy didn't know, who had beady eyes and an odd little moustache. It wasn't Herr Bayer, but Freddy thought it might be his father, or maybe a former headmaster. And in front of him at the end of the office, in front of the window that marked the middle of the school building and overlooked the playground, sat Herr Bayer on a tall chair behind a grand desk. Freddy reckoned he was probably about the same age as his father, maybe a bit older, and as the bald, bespectacled man lifted himself from his chair, he beckoned Freddy to come and sit on one of the much smaller, green leather-upholstered seats on the other side of the desk. Freddy inched towards the chair and eased himself in, unsure whether he should speak first or wait for Herr Bayer to break the silence.

"We haven't met properly before, have we Stern?" Herr Bayer said, removing the glasses from his nose and placing them upside down on the desk infront of him.

Freddy was unable to decipher his tone and couldn't tell whether he was in trouble or not.

"As you know, I am the headmaster of this school, but what may surprise you is that I am also a friend of your father," continued Herr Bayer, not waiting for a response. "I asked him not to mention it to you as I didn't want anybody to think you may get favourable treatment, but I am a member of the same gymnastics club and I have always been impressed by your father's ability to run the club so efficiently, not to mention his warmth and generosity to our members. Over the years, we have become friendly and have often travelled together to tournaments outside of Montabaur. I was saddened when he resigned from his position in the summer. The club hasn't been the same since, and I'm ashamed to say I haven't made enough of an effort to see him and check how he's doing."

Freddy had no idea his father was no longer president of the gymnastics club. He hadn't said anything, and as far as he knew, his dad still went to the club at evenings and weekends. Although now that Freddy thought about it, the frequency of his visits had dropped considerably, and his father seemed to have been spending more time in his workshop.

Herr Bayer continued, lowering his voice, "The reason I called you here today is very important. As headteacher of this school, I am involved in local and regional governmental meetings. I hear a lot about what the Nazis are planning. Listen to me very carefully now, Stern. You mustn't tell anybody about what we discuss in this meeting. If any of your friends ask, tell them I wanted to talk to you about your poor grades in music, ok?"

Freddy nodded but didn't have time to respond before Herr Bayer continued.

"Things are changing. Germany is changing. It is no longer

safe for you. For your people. You need to tell your parents to try and find a way to leave Germany. It will be for the best. Do you understand?"

Again, Freddy nodded but didn't really understand why Herr Bayer was telling him this or what it meant.

The headmaster cleared his throat, "Ok, you may go."

And with as much trepidation as he had when entering the headmaster's office, Freddy picked up his bag and walked back out.

It was breaktime, and Freddy walked out of the school building into the playground, looking back over his shoulder, up at the balcony and window of Herr Bayer's office. He scanned the playground, looking for Zimmermann, and clocked him reading a book on a bench under the large oak tree in the corner. Vögel had been slowly drifting apart from the group. Since his summer at the Hitler Youth camp, he had spent more and more time with Horst Fuchs and his gang, spending weekends at Nazi rallies and completing training drills in the forests around town. Although there had not been any major disagreement between them, Freddy had sensed that it was because of him that Vögel had moved on from the group and felt a sense of guilt about it, even though he knew deep down that he had not done anything wrong.

Freddy arrived at the bench where Zimmermann sat and looked down at his friend, sitting quietly, reading.

"Hey Josef," he said, "what are you reading?"

Zimmermann lifted his eyes to look up at Freddy without moving his head, then looked back down at his book, all the while without saying a word. Slowly, he closed the book and stood up so that his eyes briefly met Freddy's before looking back down towards the floor.

"I'm sorry, Fred," Zimmermann said. "My dad said I'm not allowed to talk to you anymore."

As he walked away back towards the school, he took a small piece of paper out of his pocket and pushed it into Freddy's hand.

Freddy watched his friend walk away, unable to speak and not knowing what to think. He stood under the oak tree, rooted to the spot, frozen in both body and mind, not knowing how to try to even begin processing what had just happened. Making it to the bench on which Zimmermann had been sitting moments earlier, Freddy sat down and opened the note. The yellowed piece of paper, which was tightly folded, felt almost crisp in the cold of the day, and Freddy noticed his hands were trembling as they unfolded each crease. Inside, written in the familiar untidy scrawl of his friend, no, former friend, Josef Zimmermann, Freddy read.

Dear Fred,

I'm sorry. My Dad says that I can't speak to you anymore because you are Jewish, and it might bring trouble to me and our family. Maybe we can try and communicate through these notes instead? We can leave them for each other in the hole in the oak tree.

I deeply wish things could be different. Perhaps in the future, things might be normal again.

Take care,

Josef.

A tear rolled down Freddy's cheek and into his mouth. The saltiness encapsulated his mood and brought a moment of comfort. First, Rudi and Gabsy had left. Then, Vögel had gone over to Fuchs' gang. And now Zimmermann. Awkward, podgy, geeky, but funny, interesting and warm-hearted Zimmermann. Freddy knew the decision had been taken out of his friend's hands and that he had probably been as reluctant to end their friendship as Freddy was to receive the news about it. But even so, it hurt. Freddy felt alone. So, so alone as the drizzle of the cold autumn afternoon hit his face and he realised all the other children had already left the playground to stay dry. He thought how glad he was at least to have Landau, trusty Landau, who'd slept at the end of his bed every night since they returned from Herborn, despite the protests from his mother. Each day when Freddy returned home from school, Landau was waiting at the top of the staircase to greet him and welcome him. Right now, that's what he needed. He stood up from the bench, and in the middle of the day, Freddy walked out of the school gates and headed home through the increasingly heavy rain, back to Landau.

As Freddy approached the house, he saw his father standing outside on the step, shouting at a man he had not seen before.

"You take your derisory offer and shove it," shouted Meyer. "My business and my home are not for sale!"

The stranger was dressed in a long, black, leather coat that reached down to his shins and had a swastika armband around the left arm. Tall and with a strikingly angular face, he looked agitated and angry.

"You'll be sorry!" he retorted coldly. "If you think my offer today was derisory, just wait until tomorrow!" He walked away, past Freddy, the rain dripping off his coat like bullets deflecting off a shield and his boots clacking on the pavement as he marched off.

Freddy entered the workshop and could immediately tell how tense his father was, worse than after any prank he'd pulled. He thought it best not to enquire who the mysterious stranger was, so he mumbled a quick greeting in a low monotone and walked straight through the workshop towards the back staircase. Meyer was so worked up that he didn't acknowledge his son and hadn't even realised that he had returned from school hours earlier than he should have. With his dad in this kind of mood, Freddy thought better of discussing his conversation with Herr Bayer or the note from Zimmermann with him. Instead, he continued up the steep stairs, turning and sitting on the top step when he reached the summit. Still with his soaking wet coat and satchel on, Freddy lay down on the floor, his feet on the stairs below, and stared straight up at the ceiling. Without flinching, and with no desire to move, he lay there and let Landau lick away at his face.

5. KRISTALLNACHT
NOVEMBER 1938

Freddy woke with a start, his eyes and ears tuning in quickly to his environment. Even though his bedroom faced the back of the house, he was sure he could hear shouting coming from outside. Then it came. Smash! Whatever it was it sounded *really* close. He sat up in his bed, the hairs on the back of his neck stood up and a shiver spread across his whole body. *What on earth is going on?* His bedroom door burst open, and his mother rushed in, quickly taking the dressing gown from the hook on the back of the door and thrusting it at Freddy, urging him to get up and put it on. With one arm in and one arm still struggling to find the sleeve, his mother grabbed his hand and yanked him out of the bedroom into the hallway, where she dragged the large trunk from under the coat hooks into the middle of the hall, right in front of the staircase. She stepped up onto the top of the trunk and pulled Freddy up with her, lifting him up so that he could reach the hatch in the ceiling.

"Quickly, quickly," she urged as Freddy lifted and pushed the hatch aside before hoisting himself up through the hole and into the space above. Freddy looked down on his mother below, awkwardly jumping off the trunk and pushing it back into place at the side of the hallway.

"Be silent and still until I come and get you," she said, looking back up at him. "Go! Go!" she urged.

With that, Freddy moved the cover back over the hatch, sealing himself into the dark loft.

The moonlight beamed in through the small windows in the slanted ceiling, and as Freddy crept towards them, he could tell it must be late because the sky above was jet black, cloudless and had a very eerie feel to it. The shadow cast from the window against the wall at the back of the attic felt almost haunted and Freddy kept turning to look at it, feeling like he was accompanied by some kind of supernatural being. Slowly, Freddy rose up to look out the window. He looked down at the street below, spotting the source of the shouting he'd heard moments earlier from his bedroom. There were lots of people outside, including neighbours he recognised, policemen and soldiers. Some were running along the street, some were just standing around, observing what was going on. He noticed Herr Motzi, the local beggar now looking smart, dressed in a Nazi uniform directing a gang of Hitler Youth cadets to set bonfires in the middle of the road.

Beneath him, right outside his father's shop, were around twenty people, shouting, clapping and laughing. It was hard to see what was taking place from the angle of the window, but it looked like these people were taking the hides, tools and products from the shop and throwing them onto one of the bonfires. As Freddy's eyes focused in, he recognised the angular face and striking features of the man his father had been arguing with when he returned from school the previous day. And there, standing next to him, cackling and grinning with pleasure as the flames from the bonfire

51

illuminated his face, was Horst Fuchs.

Freddy continued to survey the scene. He saw similar fires burning all along Bahnhofstrasse with crowds of differing sizes grouped outside what appeared to be all of the Jewish homes and businesses. Across the street, outside Blumenthal's furniture store, he could see the shop window had been smashed and a Star of David, together with the word "JEW" had been daubed in red paint on the wall outside. People carried all sorts of items; tables, chairs and other soft furnishings, out through the hole where the window had been and were piling the furniture up in the middle of the road. And if Freddy wasn't mistaken, one of those people was his old friend, Adolf Vögel.

As Freddy tried to avert his eyes from the scene of chaos below him, he began to wish he hadn't. Casting his eyes up towards the sky, he noticed a bright hue that he initially thought was the illumination of the moon. But he soon realised it was something very, very different. A striking orange light, deep and vibrant in colour was rising behind the brick spire of the Montabaur synagogue. The roof of the building was on fire, and Freddy could see the blaze bursting through the tiles, revealing blackened beams and flames, *so* many flames, dancing as if in ridicule, and yet, he couldn't stop watching.

He was snapped from his trance by a shrill, piercing scream that seemed to get louder and louder. The street stole his attention again, giving a haunting scene, the likes of which he could never have imagined. Frau Kahn, a lady he knew from synagogue and a friend of his parents, was being dragged down the street by a policeman who had hold of her long, silver-grey ponytail. Dressed only in her nightgown against the cold November night, her feet scraped along the cobbles behind her. As she tried to support herself with her hands, her tormentor showed no mercy, nor cared for her screams as he dragged her towards the train station.

Tears were streaming down Freddy's face as the stark reality of what was happening outside found clarity in his mind. A loud bang and heavy footsteps coming up the staircase into the flat drew him away from the window, and as quietly as he could, he lay down on the floor of the loft, pressing his ear to the hard, cold floor boards to try and hear what was happening in the flat beneath him. There was so much noise that it was hard to make out what was going on. He could hear what seemed like many different footsteps coming in and out of the various rooms, furniture being moved around carelessly, things being thrown, glass being smashed and, above all of it, Landau barking incessantly.

Freddy pressed his ear harder to the floor and heard a man's voice asking curtly, "Where is the boy?"

"He's not here," he heard his mother reply. "He's staying with his grandparents in Herborn."

"Where. Is. The. Boy?" the man asked again, this time

even more sharply.

"I told you, he's not here. He's in Herborn," came his mother's response before Freddy heard a scream and then a thud.

More footsteps and another man's voice, slightly higher in tone, could be heard. "The boy's room is empty. The bed hasn't been slept in," he said.

She must have made up my bed.

"Take them outside," he heard the first man say, "and shut that dog up!"

Footsteps and shuffling rifled below as the people moved out of the flat and down the stairs to the workshop, followed by three very loud thuds, after which Landau stopped barking and everything in the house seemed to go silent. Lifting himself gently off the floor, Freddy moved back to his spot at the loft window and saw his parents, flanked by police, stumbling out of their house and into the street. His father appeared to be limping, and his mother was holding the left side of her face. As his parents were directed away from their home and down the street, the crowd outside began to jeer, shout and kick at them. Freddy couldn't understand how the people who had, until recently, been their neighbours, acquaintances and friends could behave like his. The man he now assumed to be Herr Fuchs approached his father, said a few words to him and then spat in his face before directing the policemen to take them towards the train station.

With his head in a spin, and a feeling of sickness in the pit of his stomach, Freddy sat down on the floor, drawing his knees into his chest and cradling them, crying silently as he rocked back and forth, trying to blot the images he had just witnessed from his mind.

What on earth is going on?

What on earth is going on?

What on earth is going on?

Freddy opened his eyes, stirred by a dull, musty light sinking in from the window and by the sound of raindrops dripping gently onto the roof above him. Everything else seemed to be silent. As the horrors of the previous night quickly returned to his mind, he pressed his ear to the floorboards and listened intently for what felt like an hour, but there was no sound coming from below. Slowly, he stood up and looked out of the window from where he had watched the chaos unfold. The street below was now empty, save for the smouldering pyres of charred furniture, books, clothing and other belongings, along with the shattered glass littering the areas in front of Jewish homes.

With trepidation in his fingers and a sudden prickly sweat coming over his forehead, he lifted the cover on the hatch and listened again to double check the flat was empty. Then, without the benefit of the trunk beneath him to limit the drop to the floor, Freddy sat on the edge of the opening, putting his feet through, and lowered himself down as much as he could before dropping the six feet or more down to the floor below. He stood, frozen, surveying the disarray and damage around him. Their flat, his home, had been ransacked. Trashed. Cupboards and drawers had been emptied, furniture upturned, glasses, vases and ornaments smashed. Even the piano, which had belonged to his grandmother, had been demolished. He saw the frame in which his father's war medals had once hung proudly, shattered into many pieces with the medals nowhere to be seen.

Walking into the kitchen, however, he came across the most distressing sight, which made him vomit. He now understood why Landau had stopped barking so suddenly. Poor, innocent, wonderful Landau, who had provided him with such incredible friendship when his cousins and other friends had either abandoned or turned on him. The one being that Freddy had come to trust, rely on and confide in. Suddenly, he couldn't bear to be in the flat anymore.

He got dressed and found a small backpack that he had used for day trips to the countryside and filled it with a few items of clothing, a pocket knife his grandfather had given him for his last birthday and a few photographs of his parents, himself with Rudi and Gabsy, and one of Landau. Still stuffing everything into his bag as he ran down the stairs and out of the back door, he pulled his bicycle out of the shed, opened the back gate and cycled away from Montabaur as fast as he could.

6. CHANUKAH
DECEMBER 1938

"Baruch atah adonai eloheinu melech ha-olam, asher kid'shanu b-mitzvotav, v'tzivanu l'hadlik ner shel Chanukah."

Papa David said the blessing and Freddy lit the silver menorah, one candle at a time. As he did so, the room grew brighter, bringing light and warmth into the family's home. It drew an envelope of calm over Freddy, the first time he had felt this positive in weeks. He surveyed the spread of traditional sufganiot and delicious potato latkes his mother and grandmother had prepared. For the others in the room, however, they were still very much on their guard. Grandma Rosa checked the shutters against the window behind her, ensuring they were fully closed and that the menorah's light couldn't seep out, giving away the fact the family were breaking German law by marking the Jewish festival.

"Do you know why we celebrate Chanukah, Freddy?" his grandfather asked.

"Because the Maccabees defeated the Assyrian army, and when they went to the temple to light the holy candles, the oil they found should have lasted only one day. But a miracle happened, and it lasted for eight days." Freddy replied confidently. "Rabbi Zeitlin told us in Sunday School."

"Ach," came his grandfather's knowing reply, "such a clever boy! That is correct, and you did very well to remember it, but there is another lesson from the Chanukah story that we need to remember. Look at the candles there, Freddy, burning bright. It reminds us that from darkness, comes light. That good overcomes evil. And that from despair, comes hope."

Freddy looked up at his grandfather. Illuminated by the candlelight, he looked really old as the wrinkles on his face became more prominent, highlighted by the shadows. Freddy could only give a weak nod, not really understanding how else he should respond.

It had been four weeks since Kristallnacht, and Freddy had not returned to the family's home in Montabaur since he had jumped on his bicycle and cycled the seventy kilometres to his grandparents' farm in Herborn, where the action against the Jews had been far less severe. His mother had been held in state custody for three days and had made her way there, too, after she had been released. But there had been no sign or word of his father, and with every day that passed, the family became more and more concerned for him.

And then it came. A knock at the door. Everyone froze, a permeating shiver of fear engulfing each person in the room and a cold sweat instantly rising to their skins.

A second knock came.

Papa David moved first, blowing out the Chanukah

candles and ushering his family into the corner of the room, hopeful that the shadows there may offer some protection from whatever darkness may be at their door.

The door of the farmhouse seemed to close as soon as it had opened, and Papa David reappeared in the doorway to the parlour where the rest of the family were cowering.

"Freddy, go to your room," he said solemnly.

"But ... we haven't even had our latkes yet."

"Freddy, go to your room," Papa David repeated.

Freddy could tell this was not a time to argue, and took himself begrudgingly out of the parlour and into the hallway where the staircase was. But instead of following his grandfather's orders and going to his room, he remained at the bottom of the stairs, listening.

He could hear his mother sobbing, uncontrollably at first, but as she began to regain her composure, he heard another voice. A male voice. Slow and shaky. Slightly different to how he remembered it, but overwhelmingly familiar. It was his dad. His dad was back.

"From the station in Montabaur, they put us on a train to Frankfurt, where we were transferred into cattle wagons. There were hundreds of men in each carriage, with no space to sit down, and just a bucket in the corner for a toilet. Such conditions would not be suitable for animals, never mind humans. We were locked in this carriage all night, shivering in the freezing cold with just the breath of our fellow prisoners for warmth. No food or water. In the morning, the train began to move, and after a number of hours, we arrived at Erfurt, where we were herded from the train into trucks which took us on the final leg of the journey to the prison. A place called Buchenwald. Don't be fooled by the name, it was no holiday camp. As we disembarked from the trucks, I noticed a sign above the gate which read "Every Man for Himself." This was an ominous sign of what was to come.

"On arrival, we were marched into a large yard. I noticed dried blood stains in various places on the ground. There were SS guards lined up with dogs straining on their leashes, barking at us as though we were prime steaks to be devoured. We were given prison uniforms, a thin and scratchy striped jacket with a yellow Star of David stitched onto the breast, trousers and a cap. We queued at a table to receive a small bowl of thin, weak broth and a piece of stale bread and then were taken to our barracks; long, single-story huts with bunks, four-levels high lining each wall. Within each bunk were five to six men, sleeping head to toe on straw with no space to turn. There were no facilities for bathing and only a shared, open toilet at the end of the block, with rats living side by side with the prisoners. The stench in those barracks is something I will never forget for as long as I live.

"Each day we were woken up at 4 a.m., and were given a weak black coffee and small piece of bread, our only solid food for the day. Afterwards, we had morning roll call where we had to stand to attention in the yard, freezing cold in rain or snow until we had been counted. If a mistake was made, it had to be repeated until it was correct. Then, we went to work, building the camp out. I was on a work detail digging the foundations for a new building at the edge of the camp in the forest. At least there, we had some shelter from the trees, which helped keep off the rain and snow. We laboured all day, getting hungrier and weaker as the day wore on. Some thin soup was provided at lunchtime and again at the end of the day, before another roll call and then a return to our barracks to sleep as best we could. This routine continued seven days a week, without a sabbath to rest.

"After about three weeks of this, I was sought out during the evening roll call and taken out of the line by an SS guard, who escorted me to the main building of the camp. There, I was led down a flight of stone steps to the basement and put in a small concrete room with just a bucket for a toilet, and a small, brick-sized vent in the top of the wall for light and air. I lay on the cold, hard floor but was unable to sleep. After something like twenty-four hours without any food, the camp commandant who ran the camp entered the cell. I had seen him at roll calls but had never been alone with him. Without any explanation, he took out a wooden truncheon and beat me with it until I was unconscious. When I came around, there was some cold soup and bread waiting for me, but I felt too nauseous to eat.

"The next evening the same thing happened. The camp

commandant came in, beat me until I passed out, and when I came around, there was food again; soup, bread and a small piece of sausage. This time, despite the nausea, I forced myself to eat, including the sausage, even though I knew it wasn't kosher. Every day for five days, I took a beating until I was unable to stand or use the toilet. Each day, there was a little more food for me, which I forced down. I wondered why I had been selected for this treatment and when it might end but I knew that if I complained, or even asked why, I may be killed immediately. At one point, I thought death *would* be a better option than to suffer these continuous beatings, but I was too weak to do anything about it.

"On the sixth day in this cell, the camp commandant didn't come, but instead, two SS officers came and carried me out of the cell, dragged me up the stone steps and took me to the camp commandant's office. They sat me on a wooden chair opposite his desk, and I struggled to even stay sitting. The camp commandant called my name, and I summoned my strength to look up at him. When I did, I couldn't believe my eyes. Standing next to the him was Herr Fuchs, the man who had tried to buy our business and house in Montabaur. At first, I thought I must be hallucinating or that perhaps it was a man who looked very much like him, but no. It was him. Fuchs was wearing a higher-ranking uniform than when we had seen him on Kristallnacht, he must have been promoted. Fuchs gave me an ultimatum. Sign over the house and the business to him, or I would never be released.

"There was nothing else I could do. Having been at the

darkest depths of despair just a few hours earlier, I saw a chance to live and return to you, my family. They offered me one thousand Reichsmarks and my freedom. I also had to pay an administrative charge of one thousand Reichsmarks. I signed the sale agreement, and then, a guard brought me some clothes and a train ticket and escorted me to the gate of the camp. And that was it. I managed to hitch a ride to Erfurt and then came here to find you. I'm glad you are safe and well."

"Dad!" Freddy couldn't hold it in anymore and ran from the bottom of the stairs straight into the parlour and into his father's arms. He hadn't looked up at his dad, hadn't seen the swelling on his face or the bruising across his cheeks, nose and forehead. He hadn't noticed his father was stooping or that he was bearing more weight on one leg than the other. However, once the initial elation of his father's embrace began to pass, he realised that his arms seemed less muscular than he remembered. Weaker, bonier. He noticed he could now wrap his arms right around his dad, which he had been unable to do before. And slowly, as the embrace ended, Freddy stepped away and he noticed it all, the limp, the swelling and the bruising.

"Come Freddy," said Papa David. "Now, it really is late. I'll take you to bed." And he led Freddy back out from the parlour and up the stairs to his room.

Freddy lay down on his bed, trying to process what he had just seen and heard. Had his dad *really* sold their home, their livelihood, to Fuchs' father? Where would they live now? So many questions whirled around in his head as Papa David sat down on the bed next to him.

"Papa, is it true?" he asked. "What Dad was saying, about that camp place and selling the house to Herr Fuchs?"

"Yes, Freddy, it's true. We are living in very difficult times, and you will need to be strong to survive. But remember what I told you, from darkness, comes light. The night doesn't last forever, and a new dawn will always rise."

He kissed his grandson on the forehead and then stood to leave before saying, "Ach, I almost forgot. Your Chanukah geld." He reached into his pocket, pulling out two gold coins.

Freddy had never seen anything so shiny. He took the coins, from his grandfather and held them in the palms of his hands. Each was about three centimetres in diameter and had the silhouette of Kaiser Wilhelm II on one side and the German standard on the other.

"Keep them safe, Freddy," his grandfather said. "You never know when you might need them."

And as he turned to leave the room, he looked back at his grandson, sitting on his bed, still admiring the coins, and said, "Happy Chanukah."

7. NEW SCHOOL
JANUARY 1939

"What are you doing, Mum?" Freddy asked

"I'm sewing this Star of David onto your coat. There is a new law that says all Jews must wear a yellow star so that they are easy to identify."

"But why do they want to identify us more easily?"

"Freddy-le," replied his mother, using her special nickname for him, "this, too, is for the best."

It was a phrase Freddy had heard from his mother many times before, meaning she didn't know the answer to his specific question, but that somewhere, somehow, it was all part of God's plan and would, hopefully, lead to better things.

The star-sewn coat was part of the preparations for Freddy to attend his new school. Since the family had been violently evicted from their home and relocated to Herborn a few months earlier, Freddy had received no formal schooling. But through a connection of Papa David's, they had managed to enrol him at a Jewish boarding school that had been set up in a nearby town, specifically for children who had been forced to leave the German education system. As he packed the last of his things into the large trunk that had previously sat in the hallway of their flat in Montabaur, Freddy couldn't help but feel slightly excited to be starting at a new school. He had not had many interactions with other children since the day he received the note from Zimmermann, and the thought of making some new friends and being able to return to some form of the way things had been before Kristallnacht lit a fire within him.

Meyer had made a good recovery from his injuries and was beginning to regain the strength he had had before his imprisonment in Buchenwald, despite the more meagre rations of food that were now available. Freddy watched as his dad lifted the large trunk full of his stuff up onto the back of Papa David's cart, together with his bicycle, securing them with a rope, before beckoning to his son that it was time to go. Betty and Grandma Rosa came out of the farmhouse to say goodbye, and Freddy noticed that they hugged him extra tight; both had a small tear in their eyes as they released him. Freddy jumped up onto the cart and waved goodbye to his mother and grandmother as they pulled away down the snowy track. He watched as they became smaller and smaller before disappearing completely as the cart turned. Freddy looked up at his father and grandfather at the front of the cart before drifting off into a daydream.

The Jewish District School was in a large, four-storey stone and brick building that had served as a Jewish children's hospital, until the Nazis had closed it down about a year before. As the cart pulled up outside, the imposing renaissance building, now covered in snow and ice, looked scary, and Freddy's thoughts fluctuated quickly between positive and negative ones as he felt both excitement as well as trepidation. His uncertainty was soon dispelled as Rabbi Wolff, the school headmaster, came out to greet them. Rotund and with a beaming smile, Rabbi Wolff was dressed in traditional Jewish clothing: a long black coat, white shirt and black hat with a full grey beard that made him look much older than he probably was. *I wonder how he manages to eat without getting food stuck in that beard?*, Freddy thought.

"Welcome to the Jewish District School," Rabbi Wolff said warmly. Meyer nodded his head towards Freddy, who shuffled up to the rabbi.

"Hello. My name is Freddy Stern, and I'm pleased to meet you."

"Yes, of course you are!" replied the rabbi. "I have heard many good things about you. Now, please come inside and have some soup, you must all be cold from your journey."

Rabbi Wolff led the three generations of the family into the building, with Freddy helping his dad to carry the trunk and Papa David wheeling in Freddy's bicycle behind them.

They walked into the school building and left Freddy's trunk and bicycle in the hallway, before walking down a long corridor and into a large, open dining room. Rabbi Wolff signalled for them to sit, and as he joined them at the table, a woman wearing a headscarf brought each of them a bowl of vegetable broth with noodles. Hungry from their long journey, Freddy picked up his spoon, filled it with the soup and was about to lift it into his mouth when he heard the rabbi clear his throat. He looked up and saw the rabbi, his father and grandfather all staring at him.

"First, we must say the blessing," said the rabbi.

Freddy put his spoon back down into his bowl and bowed his head.

It quickly became clear to Freddy that many of the people at his new school were more religious than he was. He noted that most of the boys wore yarmulkes all the time and had payot, curled sidelocks on the side of their heads, while the few girls he saw were dressed very conservatively, with traditional headscarves covering their hair.

After finishing their soup, Meyer and Papa David said their farewells and headed back outside to Prinz, while Rabbi Wolff took Freddy and his luggage to the boy's dormitory. High up on the third floor, the boy's dormitory was in a long room that ran the length of the building and had beds laid out in rows down either side, with a small wardrobe separating each one. The walls were painted a strange shade of green, and Freddy couldn't work out if it made the room feel lighter or darker. Walking towards the end of the row, Rabbi Wolff gestured to Freddy, and they placed the trunk at the bottom of one of the beds.

"This is where you will sleep," he said. "Wake up is at 6:30, and you must wash in the bathroom at the end of the hall, there," he said pointing to the end of the room. "At 7:00, you must be in the synagogue on the ground floor for morning prayers, after which you will be given breakfast at 8:00 and then lessons start at 8:30." Freddy nodded and the rabbi continued, "I will leave you to unpack. When you're finished, come back to the dining room, and I'll show you where to go." He turned around in a very awkward way that almost made him fall over, and, with a slight wobble, walked back down the long room and out of the open doorway.

Freddy unpacked and then returned to the dining room as instructed, where he met Rabbi Wolff, along with two boys. One looked older and was taller than he was, and judging by his clothing, he seemed to be of a more secular persuasion, like Freddy. The other was shorter, looked younger and seemed more religious, adorned with a yarmulka, payot and tzitzit tassels hanging out from underneath the bottom of his shirt.

"Freddy Stern, this is Kurt Liebermann," announced Rabbi Wolff, pointing to the taller boy, "And this," gesturing to the shorter boy, "is Shmueli Wolff, my son." The boys smiled at Freddy, and he immediately felt an overwhelming sense of warmth emanating from them. It had been many months since Freddy had been around other children, and the thought of having friends again filled him with joy. He smiled back at them, and with that, Freddy followed them out of the dining room.

The light outside was fading into an early winter's night as Freddy sat by the fire in the school library with Kurt and Shmueli. They asked him many questions about himself, none of which he really wanted to answer. He didn't want to look back, but forwards to a brighter future in this new school. He therefore countered their questions with more questions of his own: "How was it being at the school?", "How strict were the teachers?", "Did they really have to go to synagogue *every* day?", "Did they *have* to do sports?", "Did they get desert at mealtimes?".

"Do you like pranks?" asked Shmueli.

Freddy's eyes lit up as he told them of the time he took apart his father's typewriter and the ensuing rage that followed. And when he glued the lid to a jar of pickles and watched his mother try to open it. And when he and Rudi persuaded Gabsy that they were being chased by a bear through the woods and she ran so fast that she made herself sick. As he spoke, he remembered, realising that there *were* happier times before the harder ones of late.

"Last week," Shmueli said, a grin broadening across his face, "when Kurt wasn't looking, I put salt in his glass of water at lunch time."

"Yes, it was disgusting," said Kurt, raising his eyebrows at the younger boy as Shmueli did impressions of his friend gagging, leading to all three bursting into laughter.

Freddy opened his eyes. He was only wearing pants. He looked to his left, and there, next to him in the bunk, was Kurt. On his right, just as close, was Shmueli. Why were they so close and not in their own beds? As his vision sharpened, he saw that beyond either of his friends were more and more boys, all dressed in striped pyjamas and with their heads shaved. Freddy looked down and there, on the floor beneath his bunk, was his father, also wearing just his pants, being beaten across the face by a German soldier in the black uniform of the SS. Freddy began to scream, but there was no sound coming from his mouth.

In a cold sweat, he sat up and looked again to either side, where he now saw Kurt and Shmueli asleep, in their own beds. Slowly coming around, Freddy realised he had been dreaming and stilled his breath back to a normal rate. His thoughts drifted to his parents and grandparents back in Herborn, and he hoped that they were safe.

Over the next few weeks, Freddy began to settle into school life and became happy again. Even with a more religious routine than he was used to, and having to pray three times each day, he enjoyed indulging and learning more about his religion, finding that he had an inherent sense of his Jewish identity, despite the fact his family had not been particularly orthodox. He enjoyed the regularity of the daily schedule and the company of his new friends. Unlike at his old school in Montabaur, there were no bullies and all the children whatever their age, would play happily together. With recent events still fresh in his memory, the insularity and protection that the boarding school offered from the outside world was just what he needed.

8. FIRE
MARCH 1939

The winter snow had melted, and spring was most definitely in the air. The school term was well underway, and Freddy was enjoying himself, he was even enjoying the lessons. Although he found the daily synagogue prayers a bit repetitive and boring, he much preferred his new school to the old one. The teachers were much nicer, too; none of the teachers here beat any of the children, as Herr Richter had done. Freddy had made some great new friends and had had great fun over the past few weeks playing pranks on Kurt and Shmueli, as well as being the victim of some *their* pranks, which he had taken in good humour. These included being locked out of every toilet cubicle one morning when he was desperate to go. It had taken him ages to realise there was nobody in any of the "occupied" stalls, as well as being duped into asking Rabbi Wolff about the special food that could be fed to pigs, in order to make them kosher.

Despite his overarching happiness, Freddy was disturbed by the repetitive dream he kept having, in which he was in Buchenwald Concentration Camp, wearing nothing but his pants. Everyone else in the camp had shaved heads and striped pyjamas, and he always saw people he loved, whether that was his father, mother or grandparents, being beaten by the Nazi soldiers. However hard he tried to convince himself that it was *only* a dream, Freddy couldn't shake the fear it instilled in him, and often, during the regular prayers in the school synagogue, his mind would drift back to his nightmares, and the happiness he felt in the day-to-day activities of school became tinged with the fear of what was still going on in the world outside.

It was Friday evening, and as the setting sun shone through the window of the school's synagogue, Rabbi Wolff was leading the children in their sabbath prayers. The sabbath evening service was Freddy's favourite. There were more joyful prayers and songs that he enjoyed singing along to, and on this occasion, Rabbi Wolff had asked Freddy and Shmueli to stay behind after the service and help prepare the Torah scroll for the service the next morning. Freddy loved having the responsibility and saw it as a huge honour to have been asked to help while the rest of the school filed out into the dining room for their traditional dinner of roasted chicken and potatoes, the only meal of the week where they were served meat. Together with Shmueli and Rabbi Wolff, they carefully rolled the aged parchment of the scroll into the correct position so that the text to be read in the morning's service was centred. Then, they rolled it back up and placed it into the Ark, a cupboard with a curtain frontage where the holy scrolls were kept.

After dinner, the tables and benches in the dining room were pushed to the side, and the revelry continued with singing and dancing. Rabbi Wolff pulled out an accordion, and Shmueli had a small violin, while another girl who Freddy didn't know joined in with a clarinet. They played and danced for hours until Freddy's feet hurt, his ears were ringing from the music and his face was aching from the constant smiling. That night, Freddy lay in bed, tired but still smiling, and hummed to himself the "Sabbath Bride" song, that he had earlier been dancing to, until he fell asleep. But still, the nightmare came.

This time, the boys were asleep in their Buchenwald bunks, though Freddy was awake. He saw Shmueli and Kurt there, as well as a number of other boys he knew from the school, all wearing the same striped pyjamas with a yellow Star of David crudely stitched onto the front. But this time, there was no sign of any of his family. No Dad or Mum. No Grandma Rosa or Papa David. Instead, as Freddy lay in his bunk, crammed in between his friends, a black smoke rose up from the floor and began to engulf them. As the smoke swirled around, flirting with his nostrils, Freddy saw flames, big, bright orange flames, like those he had seen on Kristallnacht burning through the roof of the synagogue in Montabaur. The flames grew larger and larger until they began to tickle Kurt and Shmueli on either side of him, but they just slept. Again, Freddy tried to scream out, but no sound came. He woke up with a start, and as he sat up in his bed in the dormitory, he could still smell the smoke he had imagined.

As Freddy came round, he realised this wasn't a dream. There *was* actually smoke in the dormitory.

"Kurt," he called to his friend in the next bed. "Kurt!"

Kurt stirred and looked over at his friend. "What is it?"

"Can you smell smoke?" Freddy asked.

Kurt drew a few deep breaths and then shot up.

"Come on, get dressed," he said. "Quickly, we need to wake everyone."

Between them, the two boys ran up and down the long row of beds, waking all the other boys and urging them up. They dressed quickly, and Freddy put on his coat and shoes, grabbing his pocketknife and slipping it into his pocket as he raced out of the dormitory with Shmueli and Kurt on his tail. As they ran out of the open doorway and towards the staircase, they could see thick, black smoke rising up the stairs, and standing there with the rest of the boys from the dormitory, they tuned into the screams of panic and fear rising from lower down in the school; screams, shouting and, then, the barking of dogs.

"Come on," said Kurt. "Let's take the back stairway."

The throng of boys ran back down the length of the dormitory, through the bathrooms and down towards the back staircase. As they descended, the noise became noticeably louder, and the smell of acrid smoke grew stronger. When they reached the ground floor, they made their way out to the back of the building, where they were met with absolute chaos, stirring in Freddy the horrific memories of Kristallnacht just a few months earlier.

The seventy or so residents of the school, pupils and teachers alike, were scattered around the garden, some shouting, some crying and some just too scared to even move at all. In the middle of the lawn, right behind the school, was a bonfire, onto which men in German uniforms were throwing books, furniture and some other items that Freddy couldn't make out through the darkness of the night. Some of the men had dogs, large German Shepherds that were almost as big, if not bigger, than some of the smaller children. Freddy was snapped out of his trance by Rabbi Wolff who grabbed his shoulder and asked if he had seen Shmueli. Without saying a word, Freddy pointed to where Shmueli was standing, under a tree, trying to stay as far away from the men as possible. The rabbi grabbed Freddy's arm and pulled him over towards the tree with him, where Shmueli embraced his father and buried his head deep into his ample belly.

The noise increased dramatically as the uniformed men began to cheer and shout, whooping and applauding with glee. Freddy looked up to see one of the soldiers walking out of the burning school building, carrying a Torah scroll, which was also on fire. Freddy recognised it as the scroll he had, earlier that evening, carefully rolled into place for the service the next morning. He assumed the soldiers would attempt to put out the burning scroll, if only out of some kind of respect, but they gathered round, laughing as the scroll burned. As it became too hot to handle, it was thrown onto the pyre of the bonfire.

Even though his family had never been particularly

observant, even though this more religious lifestyle was still a relatively new thing for Freddy, he felt an immense sense of sadness and loss as he watched small pieces of burning parchment fly up into the air on the heat of the fire, singed at their edges, and then slowly float back down into the ashen earth.

Once the soldiers had come down from their ecstatic high of burning the Torah scroll, the mood quickly changed. Having ransacked and torched the building and its contents, the attention turned to those who had escaped from it.

The shouting and barking intensified again as the men began to herd the people who were huddled across the garden into groups, forming them into lines. There was one line for the adults, one for the older boys and one for the younger boys and girls. Shmueli screamed as he was torn from his father's body, the rabbi taking a crack across his face with a wooden baton as punishment for not releasing his son sooner.

Freddy stood in the line and whispered to Kurt in front of him, "I'm scared. Do you think we're going to die?"

"I don't know," replied his friend. "I really don't know."

Crying and sobbing came from all three rows of people as the soldiers marched up and down, ensuring the rows were straight and instructing the children to be quiet. The adults were taken first, with Rabbi Wolff insisting on leading the line, not out of arrogance but out of bravery. Together with Frau Wolff, the teachers, cooks and grounds staff, they tried their best to calm the children they were leaving behind, telling them they would meet them at the police station and that everything would be ok, even though they did not know if this would be true. As he watched the adults being marched around the front of the school and down the driveway towards the school gate, and with his father's recent experience in Buchenwald fresh in his mind, Freddy wondered if they were actually being taken to the police station... or somewhere else.

Next was Freddy's group of older boys, with a soldier at either end and one more in the middle of the line.

"March!"

The children obliged. As the line of older boys filed past the younger children, Freddy saw Shmueli, who glanced up at him. His eyes streaked red, and his bottom lip trembled, tears streamed down his cheeks. Freddy looked back at him, pursed his lips tightly together and nodded. He didn't know what else to do.

They walked out of the school gate and, under the cover of darkness, moved slowly and silently in a perfect line towards the centre of the town. After around five minutes, there seemed to be some commotion coming from the line of younger children behind, and Freddy was sure he could hear Shmueli's voice crying and pleading with the guard.

"Halt!" screamed the soldier at the back of his own line.

As Freddy looked over his shoulder, he saw that the guard

was distracted by whatever was happening behind. Bringing his head back around to the front, he saw a narrow alleyway to his left, and his gut told him to run.

Without stopping to look back, he ran. He ran as fast as he could. The cold night air hit his lungs with each breath as he went. He ran so fast he thought his body may struggle to keep up with the pace of his legs as he belted down the alleyway, not even registering the sting of any overhanging branches slapping him across the face.

Freddy followed the alley to its end, crossed a road and jumped over a fence into the park, where he found a large bush to hide in. Freddy held his breath while trying to recover from running. He didn't want to think about what the consequences would be if he were to be found. Had anyone even realised he had escaped? He listened acutely, but couldn't seem to hear anything. No shouting. No crying. No commotion.

As dawn began to rise and the light overwhelmed the darkness, Freddy took out his pocketknife and carefully cut away the stitching on the yellow Star of David his mother had sewn on his coat. He pulled it off, and first, using the blade of his knife and then his fingers to dig, buried it in the soil under the bush. Slowly, he came out from his hiding place and took stock. With the utmost attention to his surroundings, he skulked back through the park, making sure to stay under the cover of trees as much as he could. He hopped back over the park fence. This time, he stayed close to the wall, but always with an eye to where he could run if he was caught, heading back towards the school.

As Freddy stood outside the school building, he remembered the trepidation he had felt when he'd first arrived there a few months earlier, and how that had been dispelled so quickly by the warmth of Rabbi Wolff. Looking at it again now, even without the snow, he felt a lot more nervous to walk through the gates, and his legs trembled like jelly. He wondered where Rabbi Wolff was now and whether he was ok after being hit by the German soldier. Looking through the railings, the windows of the school building were all smashed out, black soot around them from where the fire had burned. He crept through the gate and made his way quickly to the small shed at the side of the building where the pupils' bikes were kept. Freddy opened the door and breathed a sigh of relief; the soldiers hadn't taken anything from the outbuilding. As he had done when he left Montabaur after Kristallnacht, he jumped on his trusty red Dürkopp and cycled away as fast as he could. Back to Herborn. Back to his family.

9. MUTTI
APRIL 1939

After the incident at the school, Meyer and Betty decided that they needed to get Freddy out of Germany as soon as possible. Having received no money from the 'sale' of their family home and business in Montabaur, they knew they wouldn't be able to afford to leave themselves, nor did they want to leave Betty's ageing parents behind to face whatever was coming.

Betty's sister, Herta, had moved to London at the end of the previous summer, and they had been in contact with her to ask whether she would be able to help. Herta had never shown much love towards her only nephew, but she agreed to help and told her sister of a scheme set up by the British government called the Kindertransport to take ten thousand German children to Britain. Herta was working as a housekeeper for a wealthy Jewish family in London and she agreed to speak to her boss to ask if he would help with the fifty-pound fee to secure Freddy's passage, and enable him to come to Britain. They waited eagerly to hear whether he would agree.

The nightmares had gotten worse since the night of the fire at the school. Every night, Freddy had struggled to sleep for fear of what he may dream. And when he did finally drift off, his fears were realised. He would wake up a number of times each night in a cold sweat, having seen things in his sleep that shook him to his core. After about a fortnight, and seeing just how tired her son had become, Betty had taken pity on him, and for the first time he could remember since he had been a young boy, she sat on his bed and sang him to sleep with gentle folk songs and nursery rhymes. As she sang, she stroked his hair, gently running her fingers through his thick, wiry locks and giving him comfort that she was there with him. Freddy opened his eyes and looked up at her. She looked older than he remembered, and for the first time, he noticed that she had wrinkles on her face; they suited her, he thought, and he was about to tell her this when she shushed him, and he closed his eyes again, surrendering himself to her caress.

"My Freddy. My Freddy-le," she said. "I am here. Don't worry." She talked softly, in a whisper but with confidence in her voice so that Freddy believed her every word.

"You are a good boy, and your father and I are both so very proud of you. You are smart, intelligent and kind… even with your pranks. I know that times have been hard recently, and you miss your friends, your cousins and the lovely life that we had before things changed. You have dealt with it all so well though. You have been so strong. I'm sorry we haven't been able to protect you better from all this evil.

"I bet you didn't know that your father and I longed for a child for so many years, and when you came along, it was like a miracle had happened. When I saw you for the first time, I knew that I would never love anything as much as I loved this small person. You had your fathers' eyes and my chin. I'm sorry about that! I never even thought to have another child after you, because I knew you would always be my number one. That I would always put you first. That I would even die for you. You could see how that caused problems, even with Aunt Herta. She was always jealous of you. Before you were born, Herta and I had a wonderful relationship. We did everything together. Even after I married your father, we were so close. But when you came along, my priorities changed, and I no longer cared about having the most fashionable clothes or best shoes. All I cared about was you. Herta was furious and didn't speak to me for the first year of your life. She couldn't even look at you! But she has softened over the years, and even though she doesn't show it, and would never admit to it, deep down, she does love you. And now, she has arranged for you to go and stay with her in England. It is a big favour she has done for me, for you. Make sure you are polite to her, and whatever you do, don't criticise her cooking, as hard as that may be!

"I know one day we will all be together again, either here, back in Montabaur or perhaps even in England. All of the family together. That is what matters most. Family. We had such big dreams for you Freddy-le. We always tried to give you everything we could, but I can see you are much more intelligent than anyone else in this family. You can go on to great things my darling. You can be anything you want. Perhaps even a lawyer, or a doctor!

"Whatever happens, wherever we end up, I will always be your mother. I will always be here to guide you. To advise you. To love you. Even if we're not together, you just need to close your eyes, like you are doing now, picture my face, listen for my voice, and I will be there for you. I am a part of you Freddy-le, as you are a part of me. Our beings are entwined. And remember, everything will be ok in the end. And if it's not ok, then it's not the end."

Betty looked down at her son, who was fast asleep, breathing lightly. It was the first night in weeks Freddy didn't have any nightmares.

10. THE SHIP
APRIL 1939

Wearing a huge smile, Meyer appeared at the door. Freddy hadn't seen his father look so happy for a very long time.

"Hi, Dad. Why are you so happy?"

"Look!" replied Meyer, and he pulled a pair of shoes from behind his back. Freddy was confused.

"Dad, those are my school shoes," he said.

"No! They are your new and improved school shoes!" His father came into the bedroom and sat on the bed. "Come and see," he said.

Meyer carefully lifted the lining out of the shoe and peeled back another very thin layer of leather to reveal a small round area that had been hollowed out. "Go and get the coins Papa David gave you for Chanukah," he said.

Freddy opened his bedside cabinet and took out a wooden box that had a lock on it. He then reached under his pillow and pulled out a small key that opened the box. He brought the two gold coins and gave them to his father, who slipped one into the hole in the heel of the shoe, before covering it back over and replacing the insole. He did exactly the same with the other shoe, so that one coin was carefully concealed in each heel. He looked at his son, grinning from ear to ear and proudly said, "The Germans have forbidden the Kindertransport children from taking any money or jewellery out of the country, but they'll never find these!"

Freddy came downstairs wearing his new, improved shoes and carrying a small suitcase. The official letter his parents had received included very specific instructions about what he could and could not take to England with him. He was allowed one small bag, which must only contain clothes, medicine, stationery, family photographs and some food for the journey. As he rounded the bottom step, Meyer and Betty stood in the doorway of the parlour and surveyed their son. Physically, he was no longer a boy, but a young man, tall and handsome. Underneath this exterior however, they both saw Freddy for what he was; an anxious, subdued and scared little boy. Aged thirteen, he should have been celebrating his Barmitzvah, his coming of age, but this was just another thing that had been snatched away from his childhood and instead, he was preparing to flee the country of his birth and leave his family behind.

Betty had resewn a yellow Star of David onto Freddy's coat, and he pulled it on, before saying goodbye to Papa David and Grandma Rosa.

His grandmother gave him a small packet of biscuits wrapped in brown paper and told him, "These are Aunt Herta's favourites, which I have baked for her. Can you please give them to her for me? Hopefully it will help you get off to a good start with her in England."

She gave him a knowing wink as Freddy nodded and slipped the packet into his coat pocket. He gave his grandmother a kiss then turned to Papa David, wrapping his arms right around his grandfather. Neither could look the other in the eye, a goodbye like this was too painful. Eventually, Papa David ended the embrace, gently pushing Freddy away from him and gestured that it was time for him to leave. Freddy shuffled out the door to meet his parents, who were waiting outside for him.

Freddy was silent as the family walked through the town to the train station. Meyer carried Freddy's suitcase in one hand and held his son's hand in the other, while Betty tightly grabbed Freddy's other hand in both of hers, trying to fill in the silence as best she could.

"Don't forget to write to us every week. And make sure you brush your teeth twice each day. Be polite, especially to Aunt Herta. And don't do anything to upset her ... especially not pranks! I wonder what your school will be like in England? I'm sure you'll make new friends very quickly. Oh and do send our best wishes to Uncle Ernest, Aunt Margaret and your cousins when you see them."

The train was already waiting when they arrived at the station. There were lots of people milling around, and Meyer directed Freddy and Betty to the end of the platform, where there was a special carriage for the Kindertransport children. There were a number of other families here, all wearing yellow Stars of David on their coats and making the most of the short time they had left to spend together before the train left. A whistle blew.

"It's time to go now Freddy-le," his father said kindly.

His mother stooped down slightly so that she was eye to eye with her son and held his cheeks in her hands. She kissed his forehead, and as a tear rolled down her cheek, she whispered, "I love you."

Meyer put Freddy's suitcase onto the train, and as he stood at the bottom of the train steps, Freddy hugged his dad as hard as he could, and his dad hugged him back.

"Go on," his father said, trying his hardest to bury his emotions, and Freddy climbed the steps onto the train, took his suitcase and walked along the carriage to find a compartment.

The windows in the carriage were locked shut, so Freddy, along with the other nine children in his compartment, all squashed their faces up against the window and waved goodbye to their parents. Freddy saw his mother with tears now streaming down her face, and his dad comforting her, trying to be strong. A second whistle was blown, and slowly, the train rolled away. Freddy stayed at the window and watched as his parents got further and further away, eventually disappearing out of sight. He remembered the last time he had ridden a train, when he went to Herborn with Rudi and Gabsy. It had been a totally different experience. Their first trip away without parents, he had felt so excited and happy in the searing heat of the summer. The joy of seeing his grandparents. Swimming in the cool river. Cooking sausages on the fire. Landau. Freddy felt a lump in his throat and supressed a tear, he felt anxious and worried about what the future might hold.

The train journey seemed to take forever. First, they went from Herborn to a town called Giessen, where another two compartments full of children boarded, and then, as night fell, they went to Frankfurt, where their carriage was decoupled and recoupled to another train with even more carriages full of Kinder. Freddy managed to fall asleep, and when he woke up, the sun was rising over fields as the train chugged through the beautiful German countryside. He wiped the sleep from his eyes and looked into the bright morning light that was burning his eyes in a way that hurt but also, strangely, felt quite good.

They arrived at the Port of Hamburg. A hubbub of noise rolled across the train as the excitement of the children, began to bubble over. With the additional carriages they had collected, there were now hundreds of children, all of different ages, and as the train pulled to a stop, they grabbed their luggage and made for the door. After a short wait, the doors were unlocked by German soldiers while more soldiers ran their batons along the outside of the carriage, shouting "Out! Out!". The children filed out of the carriage and down the steps. There was no platform, so it was a big jump from the bottom step to the ground, where they were immediately made to stand in line with their suitcases next to them. The children were marched, just as they had been on that night at Freddy's school, in single file along the length of the train and towards a hulking ship, the likes of which Freddy had only ever seen in pictures.

They marched about half a kilometre, and Freddy kept thinking to himself how the boat seemed to keep getting bigger and bigger. When they arrived, the children joined the end of another line, at the front of which were two desks, each with a German officer sitting at it. As the children filed through, Freddy suddenly became very aware of the gold coins hidden in his shoes. *What if they are discovered? Then what will happen to me?*

Eventually, he reached the end of the line, and the German officer asked for his identification. Freddy pulled out his passport, a big red "J" for "Jew" was stamped on the front of it. With a shaking arm, he handed it over to the soldier who copied down his details onto a separate card and handed it to him with a piece of string, snarling, "Put this around your neck." With that, the officer stamped Freddy's passport and handed it back without even looking at him.

Behind the officers were more soldiers who ordered Freddy to lift his suitcase onto a table. They unzipped it and carefully checked through everything to make sure there were no contraband items being smuggled out of the country. When the soldiers were satisfied that the suitcase contained only permitted items, they ordered Freddy to open his legs and stand with his arms out while they frisked him down, again checking for anything illegal. Freddy felt almost unable to breathe, a bead of sweat dripped down his forehead as the soldier patted down his shin and calf. *What if they ask me to remove my shoes?*

"Ok," the soldier barked, gesturing for Freddy to take his bag and proceed. A rush of air made for Freddy's lungs. He was able to breathe again.

After these checks, Freddy walked towards the ship, cold and steely against the crisp blue sky. He made his way up the gangplank, where he was met by a lady in a steward's uniform who spoke to him in English. He had no idea what she was saying, and the look on his face must have told her that.

She looked at the card around his neck and asked him, this time more slowly, "Are you Alfred Stern?"

Freddy recognised his name and nodded, and she crossed him off on a piece of paper and pointed him towards a lounge at the rear of the boat. There were many children onboard, all with labels around their necks and a lot of suitcases. Freddy dropped his bag in the lounge and then followed a group of children up some stairs onto the deck, where for some time, he watched the line in which he had just been standing dwindle through the German officers' desks and up onto the ship.

BLAAAAAARP.

The ship's horn sounded one long blast, and slowly, the liner pulled away from the dock. Freddy stood still on the deck, amidst the noise, excitement and commotion going on around him. He felt the gentle pull of the ship beneath him jar against the static of the cool air on the deck.

As the ship sailed down the Elbe estuary and out into the North Sea, Freddy watched the land shrink away. It reminded him of watching his parents disappear as the train had left Herborn station the previous day. Motionless and silent, he watched as the country of his birth, the only country he had ever known, drifted away. He felt a huge sense of relief at leaving behind the toxic and dangerous Nazi regime in Germany. It had brought him so much fear and so much pain. But there had been some really wonderful times, too. He remembered his birthday party with Zimmermann and Vögel when he had felt so happy. All the wonderful times with Rudi and all the pranks they had played on Gabsy. The holidays on Papa David and Grandma Rosa's farm. And his parents. When would he see them again? Would he *ever* see them again? He didn't know.

He was glad to feel safe, but also felt a sense of guilt that his family were still in danger.

As Germany disappeared, Freddy realised that he was alone. That from now on, it was just Freddy.

11. EPILOGUE
NEWCASTLE UPON TYNE, ENGLAND | 1994

"What's that Grandpa?" the boy asked, pointing at the large oil painting of fields with a yellow-turreted building on the top of a hill, which hung in a thick, ornate golden frame on the other side of the room.

"That…" replied the man, looking down at his hands so as to avoid making eye-contact, "that was my home. When I was a boy. About your age. It's a town in Germany. Called Montabaur." He suddenly realised just how old and wrinkled his hands looked. Had it *really* been more than fifty years since he had left there? The place to which he had never returned, but which had always held a place in his heart.

"Why did you leave?"

"It wasn't my choice. There were some bad people, known as Nazis who came and forced us out. I was lucky that my aunt was living in England and managed to scrape some money together to pay for my transport here. It saved my life."

The boy looked flummoxed. He could not comprehend such a thing. The thought of some bad people turning up here, in Newcastle, in 1994 and forcing *him* to flee from *his* home felt like such an alien concept.

"Why didn't your parents stop the Nazis, Grandpa?" these boy continued.

Still unable to make eye contact with his grandson, Freddy continued, "It wasn't that easy. They came for all the Jews, in Germany and in other places. They were mean and violent towards us, and there were many more of them than there were of us. More than six million of us were killed. It was a terrible time. I'm sorry Joely, but I don't like to talk about it."

Undeterred by his grandfather's reluctance to speak, Joel continued with his questions, feeling like he had only just scratched the surface of something that piqued his naturally inquisitive nature. He wanted to know more. He tried a different tack.

"But where did you go when you came here? Where did you live?"

"Like I said, I had an aunt, Herta, who kindly found some money to pay for my travel through a scheme called the Kindertransport. They got many children out of Germany this way." Freddy looked up briefly at his grandson who was wide-eyed and listening intently, so he continued.

"I came on a ship. A huge ship called the S.S. Manhattan and we docked in Southampton on the south coast of England. There were hundreds of children, all from different towns in Germany and we were split into different groups. My group, of around fifty Kinder travelled by train to London and we arrived into Liverpool Street Station. If you ever go there, you can see a statue which commemorates the arrivals of these Kindertransport children. From there, I was sent to a place called Margate in Kent. It's a small town by the sea and they had arranged for us to stay in an old hotel which was no longer being used and had been repurposed as a kind of boarding school for the Jewish refugees.

"I think I had only been there for around ten days when I became very ill. I had a high temperature, a very sore throat and a rash all down my neck and body," he said, gesturing with his arms.

"I was diagnosed with scarlet fever, a disease which is highly contagious and as a result, the whole school was placed into quarantine. Just because of me!" He laughed, drawing breath into the top of his mouth which made a strange barking sound, a bit like that of a sealion.

The recollection of this memory brought a glint back to Freddy's eye and he smiled, looking properly at his grandson for the first time.

"In those days, we didn't have toys or television like you do today, and for two weeks I was held in isolation, separated from all the other children, with nothing to do. I was so bored, but the nurses were kind to me and it was a good way for me to learn English, because nobody else in the hospital spoke German. I remember being very happy because news of my illness had somehow got back to my parents in Germany and they sent me a surprise package with eight of my favourite chocolates inside. I remember counting them." Freddy swallowed, and briefly closed his eyes. Even now, he could still taste the deep, delicious flavour of those chocolates he had enjoyed so many years ago, and which made him yearn for a different time.

Gabrielle came into the room carrying a tray. Freddy smiled at her.

"I hope you two are behaving yourselves!" she said knowingly, in her strong Swiss accent. She went to Joel and handed him a glass of Ribena and a KitKat from the tray, and then moved towards Freddy, bending down to place a cup of tea on the low marble table for him. As she did, a gold sovereign coin, bearing the face of Kaiser Wilhelm II hung down from the chain around her neck, catching the sunlight and casting a reflection of light which danced briefly around the painting of Montabaur on the wall. Freddy reached out and put his hand over hers.

"Thanks, Love." he said, smiling up at her. She returned the smile and stood back upright, tearing the reflection away from the yellow castle. An awkward moment of silence passed before Gabrielle realised she was interrupting something and walked back out of the room.

Freddy took a sip of his tea. The hot liquid scolded his lips in a familiar way that hurt, but also, strangely, felt quite good. He took another sip before placing his cup back down on the table.

"She looks after me so well, your grandmother." he said,

addressing Joel directly. "I only hope that one day, when you marry, you find someone who loves and cares for you as well as your grandmother has loved and cared for me. We've been married for over forty years, you know. I don't know where I'd be without her."

"What happened next Grandpa? Did you get better?"

"I recovered from the scarlet fever and returned to school for a few months before the war broke out. Because Margate is right by the sea, the British government was worried about having 'enemy aliens' so close to the coast in case it was all a ploy by the Germans to conquer Britain, and so they closed the school down. Even though *we* were the ones who had been forced to flee from Germany, we were already considered inferior here too. That was the end of my formal education, at age fourteen.

"With nowhere else to go, I was invited to stay with my uncle and aunt who lived in a large house in Hampstead Garden Suburb in London. Uncle Ernest was an economist, quite wealthy and very shrewd. He had foreseen what would happen in Germany and had managed to get himself, his wife and his two children out early and bring them here to England. That's your great-aunt Gabsy and great-uncle Rudi's father. They took me in when I had nothing and treated me like a son, and a brother. They were very kind to me. Uncle Ernest even managed to find me an apprenticeship at a company which made the lenses for eye-glasses. I enjoyed the job and the opportunity to improve my English, as well as earning money for the first time in my life, until one morning, I arrived for work to find that the office had literally disappeared. The German planes had come in the night and bombed the city, destroying the building and my job with it.

"We had a few other close calls. During one German air-raid, we heard the sirens blaring, but I had a feeling in my gut. I don't know what it was, or why, but I refused to go into the air-raid shelter in the garden. Despite some arguments, Uncle Ernest, Aunt Margaret, Rudi and Gabsy all stayed with me. They had a heavy wooden dining table in the house and we all crouched underneath it to protect ourselves. That night, the air-raid shelter took a direct hit from a German bomb and was destroyed. By staying in the house, our lives were saved.

"A few days afterwards, I was sitting in the living room, listening to the latest news of wartime events on the radio. I don't remember where the rest of the family were but I was there alone. Without any warning, no sirens or anything, a German air force bomb exploded right outside the window. Miraculously, there was a door open behind me which created a vacuum of some kind, and a blast of glass and debris shot past me into the hallway, but I was left unharmed. The bomb did so much damage that Uncle Ernest and Aunt Margaret had to move out while the house was repaired, and I went to live in a refugee hostel for a while."

Joel was staring at his grandfather across the room, wide-eyed. He had never heard these stories before and whilst the thoughts of daring escapes from late-night bombing raids sounded exciting, the soft and increasingly-croaky voice telling the tales gave away that the reality was somewhat different.

"Did you hear anything from your parents in Germany?" he asked.

"Britain was at war with Germany, and so neither we, nor they were allowed to communicate with each other. The letters just couldn't get through." Freddy thought back, randomly, to the note he had received from Zimmermann in the school yard that cold November day, pushed into his hand without so much as a word from his former friend. A tear began to form in the corner of his eye.

"It was a very hard time. I missed my family greatly, my parents and my grandparents."

"When *did* you hear from them?" Joel asked.

The tear which had formed in Freddy's eye began to slowly roll down his cheek, almost in slow-motion.

"I didn't." he said curtly. He heard the shortness in his voice and cleared his throat before he continued. "In 1943, four years after I had left Germany, I received a letter from the Red Cross telling me that my whole family had died. They had all been murdered in a Concentration Camp, a place where they herded up and sent the Jews to be killed. I lost over one hundred and fifty members of my family, including my parents and grandparents, but also aunts, uncles and cousins during this time. It was a real blow for me. I've never gotten over it."

Freddy Swallowed the lump in his throat. Joel didn't know what to say. He could see the pain and hurt etched into his grandfather's face. Suddenly the old man sitting across the lounge from him didn't look so old anymore, but seemed to have reverted into a scared, lonely and lost thirteen-year old, reliving the very worst of humanity right there in his own living room.

"Maybe we should talk about something else?" Gabrielle said, in a tone that was hard to distinguish between whether she was asking a question or making a statement. Neither Freddy nor Joel had noticed her re-enter the room and sit down in the upholstered wooden chair behind the door. Freddy looked up at his wife, he had subtly wiped his tear away but there was still a trail of dampness visible on his cheek. He looked at his wife, and then back at his grandson.

"You see," he said, "it wasn't all bad!"

"After the war ended, Uncle Ernest and Aunt Margaret bought a new house in Hampstead Garden Suburb and I went back to live with them. Gabsy had left home to study in France and Rudi had gone to America to pursue his dream of becoming a pilot, so I think they were pleased to have some company in the house. I studied chemistry at the University of London and was then offered a job at a successful chemistry company in London, working with renowned scientists, learning lots and broadening my horizons.

"One day, a distant relative of Uncle Ernest's came to stay from Switzerland. This girl had come for the summer to improve her English skills and was an incredible musician. She brought this huge cello with her and often, in the evenings, she would play for me as we sat outside enjoying the warm evenings and each others' company." Freddy looked over at his wife. The tears had gone and happy memories had once again shut out the dark ones.

"We spent a lot of time together and after she returned home to Switzerland, I went to visit her and I proposed.," he said, now beaming. "I knew she was the one for me!"

"Our wedding was in Geneva," added Gabrielle, "and it was very joyful, although we were sad that your grandpa's parents weren't able to be with us to celebrate this happy moment."

"They would have been very proud." Freddy added huskily.

"After we were married, your grandpa was offered a job in Newcastle, so we moved here and shortly afterwards Gerald, your father was born, and your aunt Bettina a few years after that."

"She was named after my mother who had died," Freddy interrupted. "It was important for me to begin to resow the seeds of our family which had been annihilated in Germany, and it was the best act of revenge I could take to make up for what had happened to me. And now look, I have six grandchildren as well!"

The doorbell rang and Gabrielle got up to answer it. "That will be your parents coming to collect you." she said.

"But I want to stay for longer and listen to more of Grandpa's stories" Joel replied.

Freddy looked at his wife, the painting on the wall, and then his grandson. "Joely," he said, "This, too, is for the best."

A young Freddy.

Freddy on his first day of school, age six, in 1931.

The Stern family home at twenty-four Bahnhofstrasse, Montabaur. This photo was taken by Freddy with a pinhole camera he was given for his eleventh birthday. You can just make out Freddy's parents in the upstairs window.

The synagogue in Montabaur, which was destroyed on Kristallnacht.

Betty Stern.

Meyer (Willi) Stern.

David Lowenstein.

Rosa Lowenstein.

Freddy's school class in Montabaur. Freddy is on the middle bank of desks, fourth from the front on the right side.

Montabaur town square, adorned with Swastikas during a Nazi parade.

The "Judische Bezirksschule" in Bad Neuheim, where Freddy was sent to boarding school.

The record of Freddy's father's stay in Buchenwald Concentration Camp following the "Judenaktion vom 10.11.38," known as Kristallnacht. Meyer was detained there from 11 November until 13 December 1938.

Freddy's passport, with which he left Germany. The exit stamps of "Hamburg Hafen" (port) appear at the top, the entry stamp of Southampton a little below.

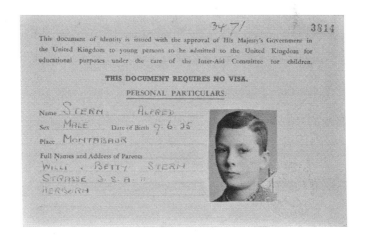

Freddy's "Permission to enter the UK" document for "educational purposes".

The S.S. Manhattan, the ship on which Freddy left Germany.

Freddy as a young man, circa. 1949.

From left to right: Rudi, Aunt Margaret, Uncle Ernest, Gabsy and Freddy, in London, circa. 1949.

Freddy with his wife, Gabrielle, circa 1950.

One of two golden sovereigns that Freddy smuggled out of Germany. This one was made into a necklace for his wife, Gabrielle.

The oil painting of Montabaur which hung in Freddy and Gabrielle's living room.

Freddy in 2018, age 93.

GLOSSARY

Adolf Hitler – the leader of the Nazi Party and leader of Germany between 1933-1945.

Ark – the most important place in a synagogue, with features like a cupboard, and usually made of wood, where the holy Torah Scrolls are kept.

Bahnhofstrasse – German translation for 'Station Road', literally the road on which the train station is situated.

Barmitzvah – a ceremony to recognise the 'coming-of-age' of a Jewish boy, usually held when they are thirteen years old.

Buchenwald – one of the first-established Nazi concentration camps, situated in the centre of Germany.

Camp Commandant – the head of the camp, responsible for all prisoners and staff.

Chanukah – the Jewish festival of light which celebrates the Jewish victory over the Assyrian army and the rededication of the temple in Jerusalem in the 2nd century BCE.

Chanukah Geld – money, traditionally given to Jewish children on the festival of Chanukah.

Concentration Camp – a prison for those who the Nazis saw as 'undesirables', often they were used to carry out the mass killings of the Nazi's victims.

Day of Atonement – the holiest day of the year for Jews, comprising a day-long fast, confession and intensive prayer.

Dürkopp – a highly respected and quality German manufacturer of bicycles.

Frau – German translation for 'Mrs'.

Führer – German translation for 'leader'.

Great War – alternative name for the First World War, fought between 1914-1918.

Herr – German translation for 'Mr'.

Hitler Youth – the youth organisation of the Nazi Party.

Kaiser Wilhelm II – the leader of Germany from 1888 until 1918.

Kinder – German translation for 'children', but also referring to the children who were part of the Kindertransport.

Kindertransport – a British-led effort to rescue children from Nazi Germany prior to the outbreak of the Second World War.

Kosher – foods which are permitted according to Jewish dietary laws. Pork products and shellfish are specifically not allowed.

Kristallnacht – literally translated as 'Night of Broken Glass', it refers to the night of 9th November 1938 when the Nazis carried out violent actions against Jews across Germany.

Latke – a traditional potato pancake or dumpling, traditionally eaten to celebrate the festival of Chanukah.

Lebkuchen – a German gingerbread biscuit, popular around Christmas time.

Maccabees – a group of Jewish rebel warriors from the 2nd century BCE, who fought and won against the stronger Assyrian army.

Menorah – a nine-branched candelabra used to celebrate the festival of Chanukah, also known as a Chanukiah.

Nazi – a member of the National Socialist German Workers' Party, which held power in Germany between 1933-1945.

Orthodox – the following of religious beliefs or rules very strictly.

Payot – curled sidelocks or sideburns worn by orthodox Jewish males.

Pretzel – a traditional, baked bread-stick.

Rabbi – a Jewish religious leader and teacher.

Reichsmark – the German currency in the 1930s.

Rollmops – pickled herring (fish) fillets, rolled into a cylinder shape.

Sabbath – the Jewish day of rest, celebrated weekly from sunset on Friday, to nightfall on Saturday.

SS – the 'SchutzStaffel', literally translated as 'security squad' was a major military organisation under the Nazis, known particularly for their harsh and violent behaviour.

Star of David – a 6-pointed star which is the recognised symbol of Jewish identity and Judaism.

Sufganiot – jam-filled donuts, traditionally eaten to celebrate the festival of Chanukah.

Swastika – a symbol used to represent the Nazi party. It was usually presented as a black cross on a white circle and with a red background.

Synagogue – a Jewish place of communal worship.

Tallit – a Jewish prayer shawl, usually worn in the synagogue with knotted tassels in each corner.

Torah Scroll – the five books of the Jewish bible, written on parchment and rolled up between two wooden rollers.

Tzitzit – an undergarment traditionally worn by Jewish men with knotted tassels in each corner.

Westerwald – an area in the central-western part of Germany in which Montabaur is situated.

Yarmulke – a cloth scull-cap, worn traditionally by Jewish males as a sign of their respect for God.

FROM THE AUTHOR

As a child, I grew up with a ghostly presence hanging over our family. Although for most of my childhood I could never quite identify what it was, as I grew older, I came to learn of my family's traumatic history during The Holocaust. The experiences suffered by my grandparent's generation had filtered down to my parents and then to me. As with many other Jewish families, this meant growing up in a relatively closed, tight-knit community, attempting to limit the engagement with the local population in the countries we lived in for fear that they may, once again, turn against us. The mental impact of events, which had occurred over half a century earlier, were still clearly visible, etching deep, deep scars into those who had witnessed it first-hand.

As my own children grow older, I began to think about how I might approach this subject with them. I want them to know about their family history, but in a positive way; where the past can teach them lessons and give a positive outlook for the future, rather than create fear and distance from the communities in which we now live.

I conceived of the idea of *Just Freddy* as my grandfather came towards the end of his life. Having known about his childhood experiences from titbits fed from various family members, I never actually heard him speak of them himself. I wanted my own children to share in this incredible story but in a way where they can create a positive impact in their own lives, and the lives of others. I want them to understand that the Holocaust did not begin with violence, concentration camps and murder, but with the suspicion and intolerance of others, prejudice and hate speech. I want them to understand that going along with the masses is not always the right thing to do, and that if you know something is wrong, you should speak up for what is right. I want them to know that as the descendants of Holocaust victims, they have a moral duty to make sure the lessons of this dark period in history are remembered and passed on, and that they and their own children and grandchildren play an active role in ensuring that such events can never happen again. To anyone.

I wanted to try and tell this story through the eyes of the child my grandfather was, showing how his normal, idyllic and integrated life began to change for the worse until it became intolerable. It started with the smaller things like being ostracised by his friends, not being able to attend school, evacuation and, later, worse. Many children weren't as lucky as my grandfather, with over one and a half million murdered by the Nazis.

All of the key incidents in this book, the bones of the story, are true and really happened to my grandfather, Freddy. They have been pieced together over many years through various snippets of stories and testimonies. I have reworked some of the timelines, imagined how conversations might have played out, and changed some of the names of the characters to tell the story.

I hope that the lessons you take from this book and the

experiences my grandfather and many others suffered through will remind you to always be kind, tolerant and inclusive and to ensure that another Holocaust can never happen again

Thank you for reading.

Joel Stern, May 2022.

AKNOWLEDGEMENTS

I want to thank my parents, Gerald and Monica Stern, for impressing onto me the importance of remembering the Holocaust. This period of our family's history forms a huge part of my identify and is the bedrock of my values.

Thank you to my proof-readers, who offered valued and honest feedback on my debut writing attempt: Sam Bartfield, Paul Boswell, Hyla Campbell, Philip Jackson and Andrew Kaufman.

The incredible cover design is by the super-talented Semnitz (semnitz@gmail.com) - it really brings the whole project to life.

My wife Rebecca has offered incredible support, both practical and emotional as I have journeyed through some of the darkest depths of my soul to imagine how the events and conversations that occurred during those times may have transpired.

I will be forever grateful to the inspirational and irrepressible Rob Rinder MBE, whose documentary 'My Family, The Holocaust and Me' lit the spark in me and helped to conceive the idea for this book. His generosity of time, words and spirit in validating my mission and vision in using my grandfather's story to educate young people on this important subject has meant so much. A true mensch.

And finally, to my dearly beloved and greatly missed Grandpa Freddy, whose blood runs through my veins and whose surname I proudly bear. You taught me so much and made such a big impact, making me the person I am today. I will be forever grateful for having you in my life for thirty-eight years and for the memories we shared. I hope that having your story told in this way finally brings you peace.

With love,

x

Printed in Poland
by Amazon Fulfillment
Poland Sp. z o.o., Wrocław
07 June 2022

1702706a-53b8-4631-8f06-b5e4bd55e664R01